When savvy gossip vlogger Morgan Sidney gets assigned the breakup of porn's most illustrious couple, she strikes a deal with her boss — if she scores an exclusive, she'll get promoted. So when the famous and flirtatious Prince of Sin offers to fulfill her three wildest sex fantasies, Morgan must decide whether she'll keep things professional or surrender and explore her sensual side.

As someone who despises the media, why is Chase Prince spending time with a reporter? Clearly, he's intrigued. But can a scorched sinner — and the biggest smut star around — let a fierce civilian enter his domain?

Prince of Sin takes readers beyond Tinseltown's glossy Hollywood Hills to Silicone Valley — for a behind-the-scenes look at a sometimes bleak, always risqué world.

Prince of Sin
Copyright © 2019 Cass Ford
ISBN: 978-1-4874-2331-5
Cover art by Angela Waters

Published by eXtasy Books Inc or
Devine Destinies, an imprint of eXtasy Books Inc

Look for us online at:
www.eXtasybooks.com or www.devinedestinies.com

Prince of Sin

By

Cass Ford

For Mum

Thanks for always being my #1 fan (even when I decided to write smut).

Acknowledgments

Thank you to the many people who supported my journey to the finish line, especially my encouraging, ever curious family and friends. And especially Amanda, Ryan and Dad.

To my beta readers — Nicole, Daryl, Ava, Larry, Jim and Chanel — you undoubtedly made this story ten times stronger. Jim, thanks for letting me tag along and pester you with questions. And to the writer's group at Amy's, your encouragement and notes kept me going.

Everyone who took calls, welcomed me to set, answered emails — and there were many of you — merci beaucoup.

And a very special thanks to the team at eXtasy, particularly Jay, Brigit, Nicki, Bo and Ailee.

CHAPTER ONE: A NEW BEAT

"I'm sorry, officer. Was I speeding?" asked the blonde temptress, her hands gripping the steering wheel as she batted alluring baby blues at Officer Chase Prince.

"Please unlock the trunk, ma'am," Officer Prince replied.

Sultry Tori Jade leaned through the open window, pressed pointy, leopard-print fingernails against his neck, and scratched gently down the fair scruff on his deliciously chiseled chest. "Can't we form another arrangement?" A crystal tongue ring glistened between her teeth.

"Ma'am, the trunk," Officer Prince reiterated in a phony, almost-Southern accent. His hazel-green eyes glared over aviator sunglasses, admiring her long golden waves and pouty, full lips glossed a cotton-candy pink.

Tori pouted and pushed the unlock button.

He stepped behind her pink coupe and lifted the trunk door to find cash stuffed into overflowing burlap sacks. Frowning, he returned to the driver-side door. "Step outside, ma'am."

"But, officer, I . . . I . . ." she stuttered, trembling.

The cop opened the door and forced Tori out. Her trampy latex burglar uniform crackled as a shiny black club met the small of her back. And as he shoved her against the dusty coupe, her cleavage bulged.

"Can you explain those bags?" he asked gruffly, his southern charm inexplicably evaporating.

Tori frowned, head shaking.

"I'm pretty sure that's the money reported stolen from the bank in town." He nodded toward where she'd come from.

"I haven't stolen anything!" she spat out in a squeaky, girlish

1

tone.

Officer Prince blatantly ogled Tori's petite figure and obvious breast implants. Parked on a desolate highway, a dried-up wasteland on the outskirts of Anytown, USA, Tori appeared lusher than anything around, and they both knew it. "I'll be the judge of that. Hands behind your back."

She obliged, crossing bony arms over a teeny, toned behind. As Officer Prince cuffed each wrist, she raised her ass. Click. Click. Next, he seized her narrow midriff. "I'm doing a full search. Who knows what else you've stolen?"

He hovered close, sweeping capable hands along her body and breathing in her ear. His fingertips grazed an inflated chest before gripping her waist. When he pinched her pert behind, she squeaked.

His hands slid up and down her right leg, hesitating atop her thigh. As his thumb settled under skintight booty shorts, Tori released a moan. He flicked a switch on his nightstick handle and the baton began to hum, its jeweled head pulsating. This was no ordinary nightstick.

Seated at her staff desk, Morgan Sidney watched this randy round of cop and robber unfurl. Scanning smut at the office was not exactly peculiar, since any subject was fair game at leading Hollywood gossip website, *Slander*.

Peeking over her shoulders, she shifted uncomfortably in a squeaky swivel chair. It might have been research, but she didn't want the entire *Slander* payroll to catch her in action. After repositioning her headphones, she lowered the volume and glowered at the screen. Attempting to focus, she wondered how people got off to such cheap erotica.

When Officer Prince smacked Tori with his ornate black scepter, then called her a whore, Morgan attempted a deep breath. But air caught like varnish inside her throat, blocking her lungs. She panicked, panting and heaving for oxygen.

Despite valid reasons for detesting pornography, Morgan refused to let sickening memories haunt her at work. Eyes closed, she practiced the pursed-lip breathing her desk mate Sean implemented during asthma attacks. Through pinched lips, Morgan inhaled to a slow count of three, then exhaled to a slow count of six.

Her body softened and she opened her eyes as the five-minute cut culminated. Tori Jade sped off with Officer Prince's cum glistening on her face. Morgan shook her head and removed the earphones to unusual silence.

A clearing throat interrupted the quiet. Morgan swiveled around, then froze, eyes wide. Nearly a dozen colleagues stood gawking. Virtuous Laura from accounting held a hand to her mouth. Producer Marcus Rodd, Morgan's smug rival, smirked. And her best work friend, fellow vlogger Sean Dupriest, broke the silence with his signature hee-haw laugh.

"Meeting in two," announced boss man Jason Gaber, bustling toward the conference room. Everyone scattered to prepare.

Morgan remained still until Sean squeezed her shoulders. "Chillax, sweetums," he whispered. "We know you were" — he paused to insert air quotes — "researching." His yodeler's cackle echoed, and he tugged her hair lightly, adding, "Nice pants. Bringing back the 90's?"

Scratching her awkward oversized pants, Morgan followed Sean toward the conference room. She generally donned leggings, comfy sweaters and ballet flats, but today the twenty-six-year-old looked fresh out of a fashion feature. Instead of its usual wild beachy waves, her thick, mid-length, chestnut-brown hair was ironed straight and pulled back tightly. Her coffee-brown eyes popped, enhanced with eye makeup she mainly reserved for work events or occasional club nights. Foundation and bronzer blanketed her face, covering cute California nose freckles, plus blush, which she hadn't worn since her sister's wedding two years prior. Sporting vintage pumps, Morgan stood four inches taller than her five-feet-six inches. Wobbling, she tiptoed into the conference room to take a seat.

Slander headquarters sat fifteen stories high in the middle of Los Angeles, though Jason would have preferred fifty-five stories higher and in Manhattan. After joining *Slander* as editor-in-chief three years earlier, he'd moved its beachside office to Century City, one of LA's most prominent business hubs. He expected employees to mimic his faux-New York City vibe, but no one measured up to his tailored-blazer-silk-pocket-square expectations. At least his subordinates had retired their flip flops.

Like every morning meeting, Jason stood beside his seat, declaring things and scribbling notes on a marker board wall. A high-end two-button jacket matched his short steely hair and darting blue-gray eyes. To exude a daunting image, standing only five-feet-eight inches, he leased customized sportscars while barely supporting two ex-wives. Adding to his identity crisis, an intern had recently labelled him middle age. Still, Jason held all the power at *Slander*, including the ability to promote vloggers like Morgan to a coveted producer title.

Two dozen of *Slander*'s most-esteemed congregated around a large glass tabletop, chiming in over a humming photocopier when needed. "Next up," Jason said sharply. "How are we covering this porn royalty split?"

"The new empress revels in media attention," Sean recounted. "But the prince still won't talk."

This was clearly news to nobody. "So, zero updates," Jason said.

Sean hung his head.

One month earlier, a colossal shakeup had stunned the court of Silicone Valley. Princess Tori Jade had kicked her man of three years to the curb, trading up for a greater crown by eloping with a woman, Viola Emperor, self-proclaimed

Emperor of the Dykes.

Clay Emperor, Viola's deceased father, had struck gold in the 1980s phone sex boom, and eventually his business, known as Clay's Empire, owned hundreds of porn tube sites. After a brief stint as a one-hit-wonder pop sensation, Viola had commandeered Clay's business after he died. In an attempt to keep the company relevant, she renamed it Lit Empire Entertainment.

Now aspiring tabloid staple Tori felt elated, perched atop the porn kingdom as Empress Tori Jade-Emperor. Meanwhile her ex, heartthrob porn star Chase Prince, also known as the Prince of Sin, remained MIA.

"Perhaps Morgan has the four-one-one," Marcus said, lifting his brows smugly. "After all, she *just* watched one of their scenes."

Everyone turned to Morgan. She glowered, certain Marcus had plotted this opportunity. Not only did he relish sabotaging her, he had forwarded her the porn link. "I was just—"

"Watching porn in *my* offices?" Jason interrupted.

"For research," Morgan defended. "Apparently it's the duo's final scene together."

"Doing your homework." Jason snapped his fingers. "I'm glad somebody around here is." He scrawled her name below *Porn Split* on the marker board. "So Sidney will cover it. Next?"

She sprang to stand, nearly falling over. "No, I'm covering Fashion Week."

"Anyone can cover buttons and frills, Sidney. I have to use my resources where they shine, and you're clearly familiar with this breakup."

"You said I could move off celebrities."

"That doesn't sound like something I'd say."

Morgan breathed deeply. "Jason, you said pick any beat. I picked film festivals."

"Marcus covers film festivals."

Through gritted teeth, she continued, "And you said, *Marcus covers film festivals*. So we agreed on Fashion Week."

Without hesitation, Jason erased Morgan's name beneath *Fashion Week*. She gave him an irritated side-eye. "Seriously? Sean was there!" She turned to Sean, who sat scanning through foodie blogs on a tablet.

"Don't drag me in!" Sean whined. "I cover recipes and recipes only. Teaser — this week's blueberry quiche is to *melt* for!"

"Our resident fruitcake is writing about fruitcakes," Jason said sarcastically. "Staggering."

Morgan sighed. Occasionally, Sean could be dependable, like his routine wardrobe of tweed blazers and chinos. Raised a farm boy, scrawny Sean had escaped the Midwest in his early twenties, discarding overalls to dress like a 1950s jazz musician. Now tall, blond, buff and worshiping his late twenties, west coast Sean embodied a self-involved hipster. But Morgan appreciated Sean's candor and investigative knowhow, despite intermittent flakiness. He'd once impersonated a manicurist to help her obtain a widely coveted quote from a disgraced musician.

"Can we stay on point?" Morgan asked, removing a stack of fashion magazines from her shoulder bag and slapping them on the table. "My weekend was squandered reading these cover to cover, then going to Melrose" — pulling the Scrunchie from her hair, she threw it down — "to buy a Scrunchie, because for some ungodly reason, Scrunchies are back." Pointing to her pants, she added, "And these *culottes*, however you pronounce that. I did my homework! *This* is my new beat." Winded, she plopped down.

"We get it. You were a duckling, now you're a swan," Jason said.

Several colleagues snickered, but they all could sympathize. Everyone had experienced Jason's too-convenient changes of heart.

"Sidney, *Slander* is a celebrity gossip site. I need celebrity gossip vloggers."

Unsure how a journalism degree led to *vlogger*, Morgan cringed. "But I already created custom Snapchat filters and lenses for each runway." Reaching *Slander*'s Gen Z and millennial audience was her specialty.

"Great. We'll transfer them to another vlogger."

"Oooooh, I'll do it!" Sean perked up.

Morgan groaned. It was classic Sean, snatching an assignment while avoiding any grunt work. "So much for *recipes only*," she mumbled.

Sean glared.

"Sold," Jason announced, scribbling Sean's name. "The fruitcake has Fashion Week, Sidney's on porn. And since the Prince of Sin isn't speaking to anybody, I need an exclusive."

Gazing outside, Morgan spotted the Hollywood sign in the Hills. Although she hated porn, she *despised* covering celebrity scandals. Taking a chance, she proposed, "If I get it, I want off celebrities. For real this time."

"Get me an exclusive with Chase Prince and you can cover any beat you desire," Jason assured her.

"Film?" She perked an eyebrow.

"Sure," Jason responded with a hand flap.

Morgan beamed.

"Well," Marcus piped up. He couldn't allow someone younger — and female — to climb past him in the workplace hierarchy. "You let *her* bargain with you?"

"Even this big bad wolf has a soft side." Scanning a pointed finger at the group, Jason added, "But don't get any ideas." He checked his gold designer watch and headed out. "I'm late for my trainer. Meeting adjourned."

Slinging her Scrunchie into the trash bin, Morgan remained seated as people filed out. When Sean passed, he squeezed her shoulders. "Sucks, sweetums. But frankly, you resemble a Beverly Hills bimbo in this getup. Not exactly your forte."

Morgan half-smiled her agreement, knowing if she traversed fashion week in such towering heels, she might accidentally take out a model and cause a catfight on the catwalk.

"Think you can make the prince *unload*?" Sean heehawed at his own joke.

"I have to," she responded. "Or I'll be stuck dissecting the rich and soulless forever."

Approaching the door, Sean plucked Morgan's Scrunchie from the garbage, then exited.

As she sat appreciating the predictably blue, slightly hazy California sky, her phone pinged. A text from her younger sister, Mandi, popped up. *Why do you keep bailing on Grant?* Morgan rolled her eyes, dropped the phone in her bag and stood to leave, ignoring Mandi for the third time that week. There wasn't time for her pushy sister's fix-ups. She had an exclusive to score.

Chapter Two: Whiskey and Coke

"Tell me you like it," Chase Prince demanded.

Trembling, the woman groaned.

"Say it."

"I . . . like . . . it," she stuttered between moans.

Inside a dimly lit stairwell, Chase fingered an auburn-haired cocktail waitress against a concrete wall. Cool colored lights from a trendy poolside rooftop lounge gleamed through the doorway. Outside a tiny round window, West Hollywood sparkled below. Chase could barely see her but didn't need to. He was master of his craft.

When Chase Prince wanted something, he stopped at nothing to attain it. Twelve years earlier on his eighteenth birthday, he'd entered acclaimed porn agent Benny Solomon's office, dropped his slacks and signed a contract that day, though Benny had never represented a male performer.

Tonight had been no different. The aspiring actress immediately recognized Chase's rectangular jaw, charming hazel eyes, bronze tan and smooth, wavy dirty-blond locks. Since she was sweet, voluptuous and clearly a fan, he offered her some blow and found *someplace private* to snort it.

Without a condom, Chase wouldn't fuck her. Even something treatable like the clap would land him out of work. So he'd settled on letting her blow him. And he came, despite taping early the next morning. Whereas less masterful performers might retain their loads, saving sperm for pop shots, the Prince of Sin always held reserves ready for battle.

Afterward, Chase teased Natalia — or Nadia, he couldn't

remember — to the brink. Hers was the fourth pussy he'd fin-ger-banged that day but the only one he wouldn't get paid for. As he pinned her against raw cement, a third finger pen-etrated her slick wetness. Thrusting deeper, he grazed her G-spot, tormenting her deviously. She cried with pleasure, beg-ging for more pressure.

Gliding in and out, he slipped his thumb over her eager clit, circling it with a professional's composure — light as a feather, gradually increasing force. Once he committed to granting her that release she craved, he flicked her swollen button with a precise stroke it had taken years to perfect.

And she climaxed, knees buckling, collapsing into his arms to catch her breath. "You really know what you're doing. This should be your day job."

Chase pulled up his briefs and chuckled, appreciating the cheeky flirtation, though not enough to request her phone number. He no longer cared for digits or names.

"Wow! You really wear BBs!" she added excitedly, at-tempting to prolong the conversation.

He smirked. His short-lived Bradley Briefs ad campaign had aired two years prior, but girls still got off on the BB Hall of Famer dutifully wearing the brand's notorious black boxer briefs. "Got to run," he said, hiking up his jeans and winking before rushing downstairs in search of an exit.

Tremoring, Chase departed a rideshare car and stumbled through a grungy Venice Beach apartment complex to enter his one-bedroom unit. Boxes of clothing and DVDs lay scat-tered. Used shot glasses, red solo cups and bits of trash lit-tered a counter and kitchen table, remnants of party days prior. With a torn L.A. Kings poster taped to the wall, no ques-tion this was a bachelor pad.

Five-year-old Cleopatra, his fawn-colored Korean Jindo hunting dog, barked and jumped up impatiently. Chase squatted to let her lick his face and cuddled her playfully. Then he checked the time on his phone. 2:30. One last shot to kill the shakes, he resolved, then bed.

Stripping off his lucky vintage leather jacket, faded designer jeans, cotton V-neck and of course those black BBs, he threw them to join the jumbled clothing strewn on the floor. Naked, Chase personified aesthetic perfection, standing precisely six feet tall, with broad shoulders, sizable hands, fine body hair and defined abs above two contoured lines that outlined a prodigious package.

Nowadays he worked harder to stay in shape than when he'd first started copulating for cash. Turning thirty a few months earlier, he'd noticed creases framing his eyes and forehead — lines gained with age and daily fornication. Still breathtaking as hell, he now assumed a more mature presence than the boy who'd entered erotica with plenty to learn.

Chase parked on a stained fabric couch, which came with the pre-furnished unit he'd leased one month earlier. When Tori had severed ties, she ditched their shared Hollywood Hills villa to move into Viola Emperor's Beverly Hills mansion, while Chase fled to Venice and signed the first six-month tenancy available.

After taking an Irish whiskey shot, he clicked on the television to some low-budget gossip show *What's What*. He cringed as Tori's face flashed onscreen. "Porn Empress Tori Jade looked like royalty at tonight's premiere," an unrecognizable host reported over visuals of Tori and Viola arm-linked, dressed tackily and overstated at a Hollywood shindig. Tori's revealing ballgown and signature tiara clashed with Viola's top-of-the-line suit, bowtie and hat.

Distracted by rumors detailing the split of porn's most illustrious couple, Chase overfilled his shot glass, flooding whiskey onto a scratched rustic coffee table. Looking down, he whispered, "Fuck" and wiped it with a shirt from the floor.

"Don't they look fabulously delightful?" the co-host chimed.

Chase snorted cocaine remnants off a coaster.

"Certainly," the first anchor replied as footage of Chase played onscreen. It started with him and Tori together, then switched to him on his motorcycle, dodging the press. "Still no word from Tori's *ex*-beau," she continued. "He's been spotted at parties but hasn't spoken to any media."

"Following such an embarrassing dumping, I'd hide too."

After downing his shot, Chase whipped the whiskey bottle toward the spotty TV screen. It crashed into the wall, glass shattering on a linty carpet.

Clad only in black BBs, Chase admired a vivacious crowd from atop a platform on one of those television obstacle course shows. Thousands of young, mostly female fans chanted and cheered from the bleachers, raising signs and exposing bare breasts, vying for his attention. In front, paparazzi cameras blinked. All eyes remained fixed on him.

With stretched arms, he leaped toward a row of trapeze rings sur-really suspended in midair. Grasping one ring to the next, he approached a platform ahead. As he scrambled, Tori appeared in front, arms folded and loudly tapping pointed-toe stilettos with a sour expression. Stretching one hand forward, he missed the final ring. His other hand persisted, gripping tightly as he dangled beneath his ex's mocking glare.

"What are you doing?" Tori jabbed. "Grab that ring and finish. The press is watching." She marched away, muttering, "Loser" quietly, just loud enough for him to hear. Then Tori grabbed a faceless woman and made out with her. Chase's humiliation motivated him. Straining for the last ring, he missed again. His free hand suddenly slipped and he fell backward into nothingness, floating down, deep into empty space.

Bang! Bang! Bang!

"Go away!" Chase shouted, forcing an eye open to blinding brightness. No curtains.

"Open up, ya arse!" shouted veteran smut director Jimmy Druck. Pounding on the door again, he wiggled the knob and opened to Chase sprawled frazzled on a couch. "This flat's disastrous. As are you!"

Through two decades in the industry, Jimmy had seen thousands of performing nobodies come and go — girls kicked off sets for snorting roxy or guys showing up still wasted from the night before — but Chase Prince was never a nobody. "You aren't skipping my shoot."

As usual, Jimmy rocked his go-to uniform of casual jeans, square glasses, a graphic tee and dark tennis shoes. His long gray hair was pulled back in a man bun — the signature 'do he'd sported back home in England long before it was trendy. A former college film professor, Jimmy had entered smut in his early thirties after being denied tenure. His buddy offered him a decent-paying gig shooting cheap erotica and making it available on the up-and-coming internet. Jimmy had figured he'd help the guy for a year, tops, score some easy dough and maybe even improve his writing before returning to a classroom. More than twenty years had passed.

When Jimmy met Chase Prince twelve years prior, he knew the kid was special. It was the mid-to-late 2000s, and performance enhancing drugs had made their mark. Jimmy had grown cynical after every horny schmuck with girth and six inches figured he could pop a pill and become the next full-frontal favorite. The clowns always cracked under pressure. With hovering crews, hot lights and unbelievably voluptuous ladies, they finished too hastily, if at all.

Jimmy had first directed Chase for a gangbang scene, with Chase as a bit background player. He expected him to be like the rest, another hotshot surfer kid with lucky length. But when Jimmy called for pop shots, as the *stars* circle-jerked themselves to near completion, Chase came on command. And after everybody else finally finished, the kid peaked again. In all his years, Jimmy had never seen anything like it. Within months, the industry had its breakout virtuoso.

Chase and Jimmy bonded over a mutual respect for mainstream film and grew close, frequently meeting at historic theaters around town to catch Hollywood classics. Quickly Chase became one of very few industry folk Jimmy considered a chum. He was also one of few dependable performers. The Prince of Sin never bailed, stayed punctual and came to set ready to work—until recently.

"Get up!" Jimmy shouted, whipping a wooly old comforter off Chase. When he groaned and rolled onto his stomach, Jimmy slapped his precious, notorious behind like a bongo.

"Can't a man be hollow and numb in peace?" Chase asked.

"Not when his cock is on my clock." Shattered glass crunched beneath Jimmy's shoes. He glanced down and winced.

"Is that all I am? A cock?" Chase sighed heavily, overdramatically.

"Today? Yes. Tomorrow? Probably. In the future? You can change that. Until then, get your abnormally-large trouser snake to my set."

"Why bother?" Chase shut his eyes and curled into fetal position.

Eyes narrowing, Jimmy stepped toward the front door. "You know my policy. If talent flakes, I don't book them again, ever. We're mates, but I hold you to that same standard." With that, Jimmy left.

Chase knew his friend meant business. Jimmy once canned a beloved fluff girl after she skipped work for a beachside acid trip. So Chase rose, showered, and fifteen minutes later reluctantly emerged from the apartment his more recognizable, crisp self. Sporting his leather jacket and worn jeans, he reached his motorcycle, snapped on a matte black augmented reality helmet, revved the bike, and sped to set under an overcast sky.

"Bob-o!" shouted Chase, high-fiving Bob, Jimmy's right-hand man. Chase often issued the duo new nicknames, like Mac 'n Cheese, PB and J, Risky and Business . . .

Meaty and aggressive-looking, Bob was commonly mistaken for a gangster or rapper. Though he'd moved to southern California from Mexico as a teenager, Bob wasn't confident speaking English and rarely conversed. When he did, he emitted an unexpectedly soft voice. As Chase entered the depot, Bob simply nodded.

Removing his gloves, Chase met Jimmy's eyes and they exchanged understanding looks.

"Haven't filmed here in ages," Chase said.

Jimmy had rented the warehouse-turned-grungy old production studio in a dusty part of the San Fernando Valley for one hundred dollars per hour. The air conditioning didn't work, and it held a clutter of random props and sets—couches, an artificial strip club stage, ladders, lighting fixtures and assorted tools. Bob left a rusting garage door half open for air.

"Repairs at mine will be finished this week," Jimmy assured, referring to his personal, more polished downtown studio. He arranged a camera as Bob assembled lights.

"What's our scene today?" Chase asked.

"You tell me. You're the gaffer," Jimmy answered.

"The what?"

"The coach, the boss man," Jimmy explained, waving him off, then pointing to a desk and chair. "How's this? You're looking for the new face of Lit Empire Entertainment, and Martini McPie will do anything for the gig."

These shoots generally followed one consistent formula: a

variation of Chase as a power player, dominating any girls who strived to please him. The interchangeable element was which girls.

"Prince o' Sin, meet Martini McPie!" Jimmy bellowed, motioning toward new girl, Martini, seated on a bare mattress on the floor. The short and scrawny flat-chested twenty-year-old looked prepubescent. "It's her first boy-girl scene today."

Martini shifted stiffly, picking at fried bleached hair and half-grinning as Chase approached.

"Hey there," Chase said warmly, kneeling down. He'd worked alongside hundreds of Martinis and knew how nerve-wracking shoots were for beginners, especially when they'd only taped webcam or girl-girl scenes. "Love your name."

She beamed.

"Your first boy-girl?" he asked, sitting down.

Martini nodded and lowered her gaze.

"I'm honored." He threw an arm around her shoulders and she smiled to reveal a mouthful of clunky metal braces. "Let me know if you need anything." When he winked, she melted.

"So glad you're my first, too!" Martini piped. "I'm such a fan. Everyone says you're, like, literally, the greatest to work with. You have an awesome rep. I wanna be a huge star, like you and Tori. Even got pierced just like her." She stuck out her tongue to reveal a sparkly barbell. "Gonna make loads of cash and buy my son a shitloada awesome toys. God knows his deadbeat dad ain't helpin' us."

Chase nodded along. He fucked about thirty new girls a year, each hungry to be the next Tori Jade. Unfortunately, most female performers were only as relevant as their remaining *first* cards—so-and-so's first girl-girl, boy-girl, double penetration, etc. Clever businesswomen preserved their anal cards to make a few grand toward the ends of their careers, after which they were typically labeled old news. Most female rookies were lucky to pass the three-month mark. He considered telling Martini the honest numbers but couldn't shatter her dreams.

"Gonna get my tits done like Tori, too." She shoved bee-string breasts together. "Soon as I can cover it."

"That's great," Chase responded. "However, let's not discuss my ex."

"OMG. That was legit savage. I shouldn'ta brought her up," Martini stammered, blushing. "Please don't be salty."

"No sweat."

"Gonna use your prince's scepter to DP me?" Martini asked. Double penetrate. "I don't do anal yet, but I'd make an exception for that toy. It's totes legendary."

Chase rubbed behind his head. "I'm not using that thing anymore." Though he'd operated his signature prince's scepter in scenes long before dating Princess Tori Jade, its imperial association now troubled him.

"Shame," Martini replied. "It's, like, your staple, or whatever. All us new gals wanna test ride it!"

"Show each other your tests!" Jimmy interrupted, referring to their most recent STD test results, a routine pre-taping requirement. "Time to let the sex flow!" He pressed play on the stereo and Black Sabbath echoed through the warehouse.

17

Chapter Three: The Gaze

Behind the wheel of a shiny silver sedan, Morgan cut across Tinseltown, through the canyon, and up to Porn Valley. It was one of those rare cloudy LA afternoons, reminiscent of four distinct seasons. Attending college in the Midwest, Morgan had experienced all four seasons. But the Southern California weather barely changed, months blending into seasons and years that rolled by with no division.

Morgan slumped. Her college days were more than four years bygone. For four years she'd worked at *Slander*, navigating Los Angeles, covering C-listers' club openings and viral promposals.

Continuing north, she passed old commercial plazas and turned down a sooty street lined with warehouses. Stopping outside what appeared to be a shipping depot, she rechecked her phone GPS.

Earlier that day, Morgan had embarked on a porn investigation that went nowhere fast. She'd quickly discovered that Chase Prince hadn't updated his social media accounts since the breakup. His miffed publicist rejected an interview request, his address and personal email weren't listed, and a call to agent Benny Solomon's office, impersonating a family member in crisis, had earned her a dial tone. Sean had finally propelled the hunt when one of his numerous elusive contacts revealed the alleged location of Chase's next shoot.

Morgan's ballet flats tapped lightly as she strode along a cracked concrete path in black leggings and an oversized vintage argyle sweater, her father's from the '80s. Hearing music, she peeked under a slightly open garage door. Camera lights flashed through stacks of buckets, mops, tangled wires and assorted technical equipment.

Pounding on a large metal door, she attempted to over-power blasting rock and roll. Moments later, Bob tugged it open. His huge frame blocked the entryway and he stared down sternly with folded arms.

A novice might have quivered with intimidation, but Morgan had jumped into the fire on countless bizarre assign-ments. It took more than a truck-sized henchman to singe her. "Is this the porn set?" she asked matter-of-factly.

"Who are you?"

His silky voice threw her off. "Morgan. And yourself?"

"Bob. You performer?"

"Me?" she answered, uttering a chuckle. "Have sex on camera? I hardly have sex *off* camera."

"Someone expecting you?"

"I'm here to interview Chase Prince for *Slander*." She pre-sented her press card, an unofficial laminated badge Jason had printed to help staff through red tape.

Bob slammed the door and shouted to ask Chase if he was expecting anyone, which he wasn't. "No media," Bob de-clared. A bolt locked with a thunderous clang. Seconds later, the garage door smacked the cement, Guns N' Roses fading with it.

Morgan stood alone under a darkening gray sky. Accept-ing the word *no* was not how she'd gone from unpaid *Slander* intern to staff vlogger in two quick months. As she examined the brick facility, which only had windows on the second floor, a raindrop splashed her forehead. She didn't mind, hop-ing some rain might extinguish some of the state's relentless wildfires, or at least end the scorching Indian summer.

Hopping over a bush, she followed a narrow alleyway alongside the building as the light drizzle gained momentum.

Drenched locks clung to her face as she reached a ten-foot chain-link fence. Through it, she spotted several closed garage doors. Agonizingly close yet so far, they teased her like Chase teased his women.

But unlike those who wouldn't hustle for a story, Morgan excelled at it. She grasped the links, slowly climbed up and over, jumped to the pavement, and sprinted toward the nearest garage door. Seizing the handle, she tugged upward, but it remained unmoved. Hurrying to the next door, she found it wouldn't budge. Finally, she grasped the third and final garage door. With one hearty tug, it screeched open a few inches. Without hesitation, Morgan fell to the dank cement and attempted to roll under but couldn't quite fit.

Defeated, she stood to leave. As she paced away, a motor hummed. She turned and watched the middle garage slide open. Such luck might have stunned her a few years back. But somehow assorted puzzle pieces always assembled together miraculously, building her stories. A pickup truck drove out and Morgan slipped inside the building.

Hidden behind stacks of cleaning supplies, Morgan observed Chase and Martini's scene. It was quiet, aside from whirring ceiling fans and the kneeling blonde's puckered mouth blowing Chase. To avoid detection, Morgan remained as still and silent as possible. Chase reclined coolly against the office desk as Martini gobbled, then he grabbed behind her head and gagged her. Morgan cringed.

"Pop shot time," Jimmy instructed. "Have her finish you."

Chase yanked his rocket cock from Martini's mouth. Morgan gulped. The camera added zero pounds. She licked her lower lip in intrigue and with a smidge of lust, resenting her body's attraction to a man getting fellated by another girl. But it had been a year since her last fling and she hadn't treated herself in months. Her clit craved friction.

Chase trailed his shaft along Martini's chapped lips. "Start slow," he instructed, "then go wild."

Tilting forward for a closer look, Morgan accidentally knocked a broom. It teetered, nearly plummeting, but she snagged it before it smacked the cement. "Shit," she whispered, glancing around nervously.

The Prince of Sin detected her slip up. And his casual hazel eyes focused on her intense dark ones.

Moths fluttered uncomfortably in Morgan's stomach. Spiders crept along her skin. But she heightened her stare to meet his cool, hypnotic gaze.

Martini continued sucking and Jimmy kept filming, but Morgan and Chase's eyes remain locked in a palpable staring contest. Who would break first?

Chase's erection amplified, like he'd pressed copy and paste, as though he had two separate dicks—one stuck in Martini's sloppy mouth, another aroused by the mysterious woman in the shadows.

When he winked, Morgan bit her lip salaciously. And with that, he exploded, literally, euphorically, never looking away.

"Get it up in those braces!" Jimmy interrupted.

Snapping to, Chase peered down. Martini's mouth slid along his bursting tip, metal braces sparkling beneath oozing warm spunk.

"Fab," Jimmy said, closing in on Martini's face, where a long jizz booger dangled from braces to chin. "Now say your line."

Martini leered, then pleaded, "So, can I, like, please be the new face of Lit Empire?"

"Grand," Jimmy declared. "Cut!" He exchanged the camcorder for a still camera and snapped images of Martini beaming, cloaked with semen.

Morgan watched silently from afar, envying Chase's release, until a firm hand clutched her shoulder. She gasped and whipped around to Bob—glaring, burly and annoyed.

"No media," Bob rumbled, guiding Morgan toward an exit as she rolled her eyes.

"Hey Bob-o!" Chase shouted, emerging from behind. Still naked, he strode over.

Morgan forced herself not to ogle his semi-erection.

"She's cool. I'll chat with her," he said.

Bob wheezed and stamped to set.

Chase eyed Morgan hungrily and inhaled her mild vanilla perfume, made more apparent next to his damp, post-sex swelter. "I knew you looked too civilian for a porn set. You're my stalkerazzi?" He raised an eyebrow.

"Some of us prefer journalist," she responded.

"I prefer invasive, meddling bullshitters," Chase trumpeted.

"I'm Morgan Sidney."

"Well, Morgan Sidney, let me go . . . de-jizz myself and you can prove me wrong."

After washing up, Chase returned topless, all abs and definition, wearing sandals and washed jeans. He approached Morgan, who was seated on a production chair centered in the warehouse, wringing out damp hair. With everyone else absent, it was quiet aside from whooshing ceiling fans high above.

"You know, I've made thousands of girls wet," Chase began, settling in the chair opposite her, "but you've lifted the bar."

She lowered her hands and huffed, then adjusted her cell phone on the armrest. "Thank you for agreeing to speak with me."

Chase slouched casually and placed a drink into the cupholder. Morgan forced her gaze from the contoured lines on his marble stomach to press play on the phone's video camera. She sat primly, legs crossed, notebook in hand. "Everything you say is now on record, Mr. Prince."

"Please, call me Chase," he insisted. "Or Your Highness will do."

She chuckled. "Mr. Prince, how have you been since the split?"

"I'm great." He swigged his cocktail, then offered her the glass. "Care for a sip? It's an old-fashioned made with seventeen-year-old bourbon. Tastes like caramel."

"No, thank you. I don't drink on the job. So, you're great? Then why haven't you posted online in over a month? Why are you dodging the media?"

"I'm talking to you, aren't I?" He winked.

Morgan faked a nauseated gag.

"You seem tense," he continued.

"So, why've you been hiding? Tori's talking to everybody."

"Tori adores attention." With a cocksure grin, he asked, "Sure you aren't tense? We could get more comfortable in my dressing room."

"Look, I'm here for my story."

But the more she shut him down, the harder he tried. "Do you do anal?"

"Excuse me?" Morgan jolted awkwardly upright, knocking her pen onto the cement floor.

"Nah, you look too uptight for anal."

"I'm not." She retrieved the pen, flipped back up and slouched, mimicking his posture. Her sweater pinched, revealing a flat stomach with toned abs.

Chase and his dick took immediate notice. "Not uptight or not into anal?"

"Both. Neither. Can we stick to . . ."

"Knew it," he interrupted. "So what *are* you into?"

"Exclusives," Morgan contended. "How do you feel about smut sweetie Tori Jade marrying Viola Emperor?"

"Tori may appear a sweet, harmless hag, but she wields a poisoned apple," he replied, taking a large gulp of his drink. "However, that harlot's free to fuck, marry or kill whoever she wants."

Morgan grinned, jotting down *fuck, marry, kill*.

"Besides," he continued, "there's plenty more pussy in the pound." Again, his eyes found her shapely tummy.

Clearing her throat hotly, she yanked her shirt down and straightened her stance.

"Midgets?" he asked.

"Pardon?"

"Now I'm thinking you're into kinky shit. Like midgets. Or hentai."

"I'm only *into* doing my job," she replied through gritted teeth.

Chase chuckled.

"What?"

"Everyone's into something. Tell me your top three fantasies. I'll gladly help you score *that* exclusive."

"My only fantasy is meeting this deadline," Morgan assured. "So I can start covering more significant news."

"Don't believe you. Let me figure this one out." His eyes searched her stiff physique for a tell. "Threesomes?"

She grimaced. Even in her last, and only, serious relationship, Morgan never divulged her fantasies.

"Shower sexy time?" Chase asked, watching.

Morgan side-eyed him. She'd once attempted shower sex but wound up with three stitches and a torn bath curtain.

Humming and tapping a finger on his glass, he asked, "Sex in public?"

A pause. "No." But the word blurted out much too skittishly. Her lips pinched. She gulped and lifted her nose, insisting, "Absolutely not."

But Chase raised his brows victoriously and broadened a

devilish smile. He knew her fantasy.

"Let me book you for a private," he offered. To get with self-important industry girls, porn stars sometimes booked private sessions, playtime without cameras. "It doesn't have to be *too* private."

Morgan scoffed, loathing him. She stared beyond his hazel eyes, which in the florescent lighting appeared two different shades. "Stop bullshitting me with *I'm great* and *Tori's free to fuck, marry, kill who she wants.* Cut your crap, Chase."

His arrogant smirk fell to a grimace as she continued, "You dated for three years. Became porn royalty together. And she publicly chucked you for someone richer, better, more powerful and connected. You're some low-grade, D-list stud, hiding because you're humiliated."

Chase eyed Morgan's notebook and camera, reminders of her craft. "You're correct," he responded honestly. "I'm depressed, so I'm drinking and fucking my feelings away." He raised the glass, feigning cheers with the air before swallowing a weak sip. "Is that what you and your audience need to hear? Royalty in ruins. There's your headline."

"Sorry, Chase, but—"

"No, you're not. It's your job." He stood. "Got your story?"

"Sure." Her eyes couldn't meet his.

"Nice to meet you." He scratched behind his head. "You're correct, though, Tori likely married Viola for her power and connections."

Over the years, Tori had desperately auditioned for countless mainstream series and never received callbacks. Stepping closer, Chase continued, "And off record, Viola Emperor is a power-hungry coward, longing for those long-gone glory days. She'd sell her widowed mother before her private jet. Wealth and power don't make people *better*. Their value is subjective, darling."

He turned and stalked away. "Good luck with your more

significant news." Disappearing down the hallway, he slammed a door.

Morgan gathered her belongings and rushed outside. Bob spotted her as he loaded a white van with equipment. "Welcome to hell," he said before plopping inside and steering off.

CHAPTER FOUR: AN OFFER

Jason didn't care where his *Slanderer*s worked, as long as they attended meetings and met deadlines. So after interviewing Chase, Morgan retreated to a café on Abbott Kinney, Venice Beach's trendiest street, to piece together her story. Sandwiched between art galleries, boutique clothing stores and gluten-free, organic, anti-GMO bistros, this café was Morgan's go-to haunt. It offered a log cabin vibe, swamped with westsiders donning bohemian beards and hemp garb. Morgan would never admit to these artists, who she assumed were penning original novels or impressive screenplays, that she vlogged about soul-sucking sleaze for a tabloid.

Although she didn't feel sleazy exposing the Prince of Sin after he'd contentedly treated her like a piece of ass. *Prince fronts as a flirtatious player,* Morgan typed. *Hunting tail is likely why Tori Jade abandoned him. But he's actually depressed and sad.*

Impressed by Chase's money and power rant about Viola Emperor, she included it to offer him an iota of depth. After emailing a draft script to her fact checker, she opened one of her favorite marketing blogs and decompressed.

Exhausted from late-night benders, Chase hit the hay early but tossed and turned. Cleo grew so annoyed she jumped out of bed to languish on a plush snoozer pillow. Chase recalled his tantrum with cutthroat Morgan and resolved that she'd provoked him. He pictured her facing him like a shark in that chair. Briefly he envisioned her alluring smile, smart mouth and darling freckles. But Chase knew looks could deceive and concluded that Morgan Sidney exuded danger.

A ringing phone disturbed his thoughts with a call from Benny Solomon. Realizing it was only ten o'clock, Chase answered.

"Yo," he grunted.

"You sleeping, kid?" Benny asked.

"Nah."

Benny launched into his spiel. "One of my girls got a call from some fact-checker, so she put 'em through to me. Did you have a fit during a tabloid interview today, with a chick named Barbie something?"

"Who?" Chase scratched his head, wondering what Benny was on this time.

"I don't fucking know who. They claim you fired shots at Viola Emperor."

Chase groaned and pictured Morgan. "What did you tell them?"

"That I don't handle interviews and fuck off!" Benny spewed. "But they claim to have it on tape. If that's true, you better deal with it. You can't shit talk the dyke who signs your paycheck, even if she's a royal cunt. Doesn't your publicist broad manage this crap? Kid, I gotta bounce. I got bottles at the Wildebeest if you want in." *Click.*

The man who represented nearly every top female porn star still paid for bottles at titty bars for a thrill. Chase shook his head, feeling no desire to join the party. Certain he'd uttered that Viola Emperor comment *off* record, Chase decided to phone his publicist for immediate damage control first thing in the morning—though part of him wanted to take Morgan down himself.

After watching young Martini McPie accept the Prince of Sin's face shot a day prior, Morgan needed a reminder that she owned her own sexuality. She took a rejuvenating exercise class and hurried to work to finesse her exclusive. In the car, she held a country music sing-along dance party to celebrate choosing her next beat. Entering *Slander* just after 9 a.m., she strode keenly toward her desk.

"Morgan!" bellowed a too-familiar voice as Chase Prince emerged from behind a pillar. "Or is it Barbie now?" Stalking forward, he unfurled for a hug.

Startled, she nearly flung backward but quickly regained composure and swerved around him to her desk. On set she'd succumbed to his charms, but *Slander* was her turf.

Chase followed, hovering.

Omigod, Sean mouthed from his desk, faux fanning himself hysterically.

"I have one hundred things to do," she told Chase assertively, perusing a file folder.

"Make me number one-oh-one?" he asked, smirking.

She glanced up as he winked. "I'd rather pass a kidney stone." Her fierce dark eyes pierced the man who helmed the industry that plagued her. Standing upright, she glowered toughly.

"I'm kidding," he insisted. "But joking aside, can we chat?"

Acknowledging the room, Morgan found numerous colleagues staring. Who could blame their intrigue as the Prince of Sin stood by her cubicle, attempting to flirt? To avoid a dramatic scene, Morgan clasped his bicep, which literally bulged, so she opted for his forearm and guided him toward the conference room.

"Who's Barbie Blue?" he asked.

"My pseudonym," she whispered. Barbie was her deceased paternal grandmother, the resilient single mother who'd raised her father. And blue was simply her favorite color. "I don't need my respected family to learn I'm covering the seediest biz on earth."

Chase furrowed his brow as Morgan pulled him inside and

shut a solid wooden door. "Don't you have someplace to be?" she asked. "Teenagers lined up to sit on your face?"

Her sass made his dick twinge. Attempting to ignore it, he skipped to the point. "Your fact checker called my agent. Could you *not* use that one Viola Emperor quote? The one I said *off* record?"

"Funny," she stated. "I specified that everything was *on* record."

Determined to negotiate, he attempted an adorable, pouty baby face. "Please. I beg, I plead."

"Oh, all right!" Morgan agreed facetiously, eyes bright.

Reading her perky, exaggerated expression, he asked, "Really?"

"No," she chortled.

His pout deepened.

"Ech. Do girls actually fall for that?" She pinched his cheek condescendingly. "Darling, you're cute as a button. But we're done here."

As she grabbed the doorknob, he tried to stop her by placing a firm, strong hand over hers. Morgan paused with a shiver and gnawed her lower lip. Chase noticed her nibbling and grinned, delighting in her reaction to his touch. She blinked rapidly and whipped her hand free.

"I could lose my job," Chase begged.

"Oh no! The Prince of Sin will lose his loyal following of horny adolescent girls," Morgan mocked. "That quote makes you sound *sharp*."

"Sounding sharp isn't something I care about."

"It's not?"

"I care about remaining employed," he explained. "And that quote puts my career at stake."

"My career's at stake too," she said. "My boss is a *dick*. And I deserve a promotion."

His dick twitched again. Her drive excited him,

confusingly because he also couldn't stand her.

"My idiot fact checker shouldn't have mentioned that clip. Stupid interns."

Chase clasped her shoulder. "That sounds stressful, Morgan."

Inhaling deeply, she breathed in his refreshingly sudsy scent. Her name flowed from his mouth like honey dripping from a spoon, sugary and inviting, though not sweet enough to pull the best quote.

He massaged her neck from behind. "It must be stressful for a smart, sexy career woman to deal with idiot interns and a dickhead boss."

"Yes, it is." Morgan unwound as his sturdy thumb expertly loosened a shoulder blade knot. "I don't understand how these morons get promoted and I—" She inhaled his spearmint toothpaste with a touch of whiskey and wondered if the booze was remnants from a fresh morning pick-me-up or a wild night out. Spotting his hand on her shoulder, she bit her lip. A tiny, curious part of her considered succumbing to his intoxicating spell and expert fingers. But her sensibilities prevailed. She harrumphed hotly and scowled.

Chase threw his arms back defensively but refused to step away. "I'm innocent," he feigned.

"Until proven guilty," she suggested.

He inched closer, backing her into the door. "I'll make you a deal."

"You have nothing I desire."

"Not even sex in public?" he answered, planting his hands on either side of her head. "That seems like something you desperately desire."

She bit her lip again.

"And your colleagues are right outside." His face inched closer, like an erotically charged magnet. "I'd gladly explore your top three fantasies."

"Top three?" Morgan hollered boisterously. "What are you, a genie?"

"Only if you'll rub my magic lamp," he said with a wink.

She wanted to huff and sneer with a bitchy side-eye while cackling in his face. But her treacherous clit craved attention. It took every ounce of willpower not to nibble his full lower lip just an inch away. Determined, she ducked under his arm and moved aside. To refrain from literally swooning, she leaned on the conference table.

His prying eyes scanned her trim figure. "You should probably get back to those hundred things," he said, twisting the doorknob. "Here's my personal number." Chase handed over a business card. "Maybe we can continue this sometime. Depending on what you decide to post, of course."

He exited, leaving her to catch a shaky breath. Through the open doorway, Morgan watched him speed across the floor, oblivious to countless gawkers. After passing Jason's office, he turned toward the elevators.

Morgan examined the Prince of Sin's card, a nude photo of him with that infamous black scepter covering his member. Despite considering him marginally physically attractive, she refused to pull the quote.

"Sidney!" Jason shouted from his office. "In here!"

Sean mock saluted as Morgan passed. She returned a half-smile and entered Jason's office prepared to defend herself against Chase's unprofessional antics.

"What's up?" she asked.

"Was that the Prince of Sin?"

"Unfortunately."

"So, you got my exclusive?" Jason asked, doubtfully.

"Yep! You'll have it by noon."

"Take the night," Jason insisted. "We can run it tomorrow morning."

"Why?" Morgan asked skeptically. Jason never waited on

potential scoops. "No need. I'll finish today and tomorrow we can solidify my new beat."

"About that. I'm keeping you on porn a while longer. Clearly you made terrific connections."

"You promised once I got your exclusive, I was done."

"That doesn't sound like something I'd say." But he smirked. "We'll run your Prince piece tomorrow. And next week you can assemble a porn industry feature. Certainly your new, noble companion can generate more scoop."

Several blocks from the Pacific Ocean, Morgan's posh Santa Monica apartment screamed wanderlust. It told stories of adventure, the walls neatly decorated with masks from India, Australian Aboriginal paintings, prints from New Orleans, Italian leather purses . . . Each a reminder of enlightening, creativity-inspiring journeys.

"You have to do it," Sean stated.

Morgan had dished about the clip Chase wanted cut, his near-seduction, her near-submission, his offer and Jason's unfair, irritating assignment, hence, her dilemma — to pull the clip and use Chase as link to the porn industry or find another way in. A teensy part of her longed to explore more, to see Chase Prince again.

"Do it, girl," Sean griped. "At least for some perverse penetration."

"I'm not going to sleep with him!" Morgan explained. "But if I pull that quote, maybe he'll score me access to an industry event or another shoot. He'll certainly owe me."

"Owe you? Sweetums, make him *own* you." Sean licked his lips. "In that rock star leather jacket. Scrumptious."

"I'm not bedding a cocky sex addict! Who's probably swarming with STDs and sports an ostentatious, *wannabe* rock star leather jacket."

Sean huffed disdainfully.

"I have to do what's best for my career."

"Do what's best for your pussy." Sean meowed and clawed his hand then bellowed that raucous laugh.

Morgan rolled her eyes and opened her notepad. "Okay, Option one." She drew a chart and jotted down the options. "Use the clip. My job means portraying the truth and my followers deserve the best." *Loyalty, not porn royalty,* she scrawled. "I'll lose Chase as a connection, but I can find another contact, right?"

"If you already have the best contact, why pursue another?" Sean opposed while filing his fingernails.

"Option two. Keep that pompous prick of sin happy, pull the clip and spend a little more time getting to know him." Morgan pictured them alone. In her mind, after his hazel eyes undressed her like in the conference room, she'd rip that ostentatious, wannabe rock star leather jacket off his sculpted body and run her hands under his fitted t-shirt. She bit her lip, imagining his.

Sean glanced up and noticed her dreamy stare. "You're picturing him naked!"

"I'm picturing him *getting* naked," Morgan clarified, snapping to and gasping at her admission.

"You totally want his man-meat!" Sean teased.

She guffawed. "Reporting on porn feels repulsive enough—I refuse to let it back into my private life."

"*Back* into?" Sean raised a brow.

Her head shook. "Never mind. I'm keeping the clip," she stated firmly. "I'll find another porn contact. The Prince of Sin is too dangerous."

"Since when do you play it safe?"

Her gaze found the framed journalism degree above her desk. "Since Chase Prince made an offer I must refuse."

"Fine, you bore. Now to me." Sean held up a Swiss cheese patterned bowtie. "Is this too kitschy for the kitchen?"

CHAPTER FIVE: LITTLE BOXES

I LOVE MY AUNTY! Morgan reread the fortune cookie message.

"Ahhh!" shrieked her mom, the jubilant Kaya Sidney, catapulting across the table to hug Morgan's sister, Mandi. Morgan glanced at Kaya's fortune, which read *I LOVE MY GRANDMA!*

"Careful, Mother," Mandi asserted, withdrawing from Kaya's affectionate grip. "I'm only ten weeks."

Kaya leaned back and beamed at Mandi, her younger dead ringer. Both women were petite, with round, light brown eyes and sandy brown hair, though Mandi wore hers longer, dyed with a trendy blonde balayage. They also dressed similarly in sharp tailored skirt suits or in-vogue dresses, though Kaya preferred vintage or couture cuts while Mandi desired brand names. Tonight, elegant gold huggie hoop earrings decorated their ears, though Mandi's were more embellished with yellow crystals. Kaya appeared young for fifty-five, partly by keeping up with beauty and health trends but also from living a considerably calm, comfortable life.

Her husband, the soon-to-be Grandpa Al, beamed and stood to hug Mandi. "Wonderful news," he expressed, shaking hands with Mandi's husband Noah. Al stood just under six feet but seemed taller, with a mighty demeanor and severe dark brown eyes that cast contemplative stares. At sixty-five years old, his once chestnut brown hair and beard were streaked gray. He dressed like a true baby boomer father, wearing dress pants and button-ups a size too large, contrasting the trendier, trim styles millennials like Noah sported.

Stepping between Mandi and Noah, Morgan reached around their shoulders. Noah patted her back.

"Really, Morgan?" Mandi fussed. "Acting affectionate after ignoring my texts all week?"

Morgan side-eyed her. "You're putting a few unanswered messages ahead of my elation to be an aunt?"

Mandi huffed. "Fine," she acceded as they resettled in their seats.

Al and Kaya had raised their girls in Foothill Ranch, a suburban Orange County neighborhood an hour south of Los Angeles. Kaya maintained a tidy, organized, well-fed home. Her own mother had paid more attention to church than the family, inspiring Kaya to be an involved parent. Kaya made time for her girls, attending Mandi's cheer or dance competitions and supporting whatever new sport Morgan took on seasonally. But Kaya and Mandi held a closer bond. Together they baked and shopped and got mani-pedis. Morgan joined an occasional makeover spa-day but mostly clung to Al.

Working his way from investigative journalist to editor-in-chief at one of the region's major newspapers, Al worked long hours and spent weeks on the road. Despite a demanding schedule, he fought to be a hands-on parent, especially to Morgan. Together they played, watched and talked all things sports. He attended her soccer matches and bought Mighty Ducks season tickets when the hockey team was founded to one day take a young Morgan to games.

Raised in New York City's working class, Al strived to ensure his privileged daughters would appreciate hard work. He brought Morgan to the bustling newsroom to observe dedicated, competitive journalists duking it out on the grind.

As a child, Morgan watched *Mulan* and promptly decided to attain something, anything successful in life. Being female would never hold her back. Around that same time, young Mandi watched *Hercules* and decided she would do something, anything to procure a knight in shining armor. That attitude followed Mandi to Stanford, intent on graduating with an M-R-S, while Morgan fled to Syracuse, intent on graduating with a journalism degree. And so, at age twenty-two, Mandi married Noah Myers, Stanford MBA and Myers Global Real Estate heir. By then, Morgan was two years out of her Bachelors in Journalism and vlogging about wig trends for *Slander*.

"Let's order," Mandi directed. "This restaurant is *the best*. It's the only place the von Troden's will eat sushi." Tonight's bi-weekly family dinner was at Ginza Sushi in Newport Beach, Orange County, because Mr. and Mrs. Noah Myers only ate *the best*. The best meant at least three dollar-signs on Yelp, preferably four, or any new spot their country club associates suggested. "Can I order already?" Mandi grasped a waiter's arm, nearly toppling his tray of dishes.

He nodded but left to serve another table.

She sniveled. "I meant today."

When he returned, Mandi ordered the restaurant's signature sweet raw shrimp dish. "They might not like that one, dear," Noah pointed out. "And don't forget, you can't eat raw fish."

Mandi shushed him and continued ordering for everyone, adding a grilled chicken dish for herself. Morgan's empathetic eyes met Noah's. Her sister epitomized the snooty humans Morgan had fled Orange County to escape. Noah shrugged.

Noah Myers was handsome with reddish-blond hair and freckled skin. Raised by aristocratic parents, he grew up alongside his identical twin in Yorba Linda, Orange County, one of the wealthiest communities in America. His black sheep brother had estranged himself from the family a decade prior, leaving Noah, apple of everyone's eye, to take over the family business and carry on the noble Myers name.

At first, Morgan considered Noah just another Mandi, a pretentious brat expecting people to wipe his ass — until two years prior, when Mandi fell ill and skipped a wild bash at a family friend's Malibu beach house. Noah drove up on his own and went shot for shot with Morgan until he performed '90s boy band karaoke while stripping, then jumped into the Pacific and made sand angels naked on the beach. Outside Mandi's keen supervision, Noah became the brother Morgan always wanted. She resented Mandi cramping her big bro's cool side.

As Mandi finished demanding specializations to the fixed menu, Al asked Morgan about work. "It's fine," she said, re-solving to conceal her new beat. She couldn't tell Christian Kaya, who preached marriage before hanky panky, that she now chronicled other people's intercourse. Nor could she ex-plain things to her father, who respected a more refined *hard* work ethic. And Mandi would simply stew about Morgan's vocation hindering her country club reputation.

"Really? Fine?" Mandi asked. "If things are fine, why do you continuously ascertain that you're too busy to date Grant?"

"Things are fine and busy, Mandi."

"Oohhh," Kaya cooed, eyes wide. "Who's Grant?"

"An old fraternity brother of mine," Noah explained, "who we are trying to fix up with Morgan."

"He's thirty-two, established, fights MMA and is an invest-ment genius," Mandi continued. "Discovers *the best* apps and startups." She glanced disapprovingly at Morgan. "But Miss working girl has no time."

"Morgan, make time," Kaya insisted. "He sounds fabu-lous."

"I'm busy," Morgan defended.

"Really? With what?" Mandi asked, scowling.

"Covering Fashion Week."

Mandi snickered and water spewed out her nose. "They put *you* on fashion?" she asked, wiping her face. "You thought Kitson was a Kardashian."

"Great journalists immerse themselves in any subject," Al said, clapping Morgan's back encouragingly, "despite their interests or fears. They take risks to get the story no matter what."

"She works for a tabloid, Daddy, not the Times," Mandi jabbed.

Morgan slinked, wishing she could produce more thought-provoking pieces.

"We just want to see you settle down, to feel comfortable and safe, like us." Mandi squeezed Noah's hand.

"So we can, like, sip merlot all day and join the PTA together?" Morgan mocked. She had no interest in breeding babies or finding her place in a country club food chain.

"Sweetie," Kaya pleaded.

"Fine, Mandi," Morgan agreed, hoping to change the subject. "If you get off my back, I'll go out with Grant."

Mandi beamed victoriously as a server placed a sweet raw shrimp dish on the table. Morgan stared disgustedly at the crustaceans' tiny antennae squirming above their slimy heads and immediately regretted her decision.

As she drove home from dinner, Al's words repeated in Morgan's mind. *Great journalists immerse themselves in any subject, despite their interests or fears. They take risks to get the story no matter what.*

Pulling into her carpark, she recalled Mandi's comments. *We just want to see you settle down, to feel comfortable and safe, like us.* The thought nearly made her regurgitate the shrimp.

Morgan hurried inside and opened her laptop. She deleted Chase's candid Viola Emperor quote from the exclusive, uploaded it, and pressed Submit. Then she reached into her knapsack. Chase's chiseled abs and too-perfect California tan rested right where she'd left them on his business card. She grabbed her phone. *I pulled that clip,* she texted, *You owe me.*

CHAPTER SIX: MAN OF HIS WORD

As Chase leaned against the Grieta Profunda Canyon entry gate in West Hollywood, slews of fitness fiends paced by. The hiking trail was an Angelino staple for celebrities, dog-walkers, tourists and even regular locals. Since Morgan had pulled his quote, Chase resolved to help with her feature. He suggested they meet for a hike because he got off watching women sweat.

Morgan strode up Flamingo Avenue in tight black spandex shorts and a loose black tank top. Squeezed into a sky-blue sports bra, her perky C-cups bounced with each step. Chase smirked admiring her physique, not missing her usual roomy sweaters.

"Darling," he said, whitened teeth gleaming opposite an overcast sky.

"Your Highness." She mock curtseyed.

They paced through the entrance gate, passing yogis practicing on a neat lawn. That was when she acknowledged his L.A. Kings snapback hat. "So, you're a Kings fan?"

"Born and raised," Chase replied, tipping the brim.

Morgan returned a disdainful side-eye glance.

"That a problem?"

She stopped to roll her shorts down, revealing a toned tummy and the brim of Anaheim Ducks briefs.

"Born and raised," she responded, lifting her brows. When the Mighty Ducks of Anaheim entered the National Hockey League in 1993, the team was geographically destined to rival the seasoned L.A. Kings.

"Do you ever go to games?" Chase asked.

"My Dad has Ducks seats. He always takes us."

"Us?"

"Mostly me," Morgan explained. "Occasionally he takes my mom, sister, cousins or grandparents . . . Whoever wants to go."

"So your family's close?"

"I mean, sometimes I want to punch my snobby sister's know-it-all face, but yeah, we love each other."

All Chase had was his Mom, so Morgan's tight-knit extended family both touched and fascinated him. In his porn circles, loving families — even cordial ones — were uncommon. Tori abhorred her parents. Reminded of his ex, Chase circled back to hockey. "You ever go to Kings games?"

"I've never even been to the Staples Center," she said of the Kings' arena.

"If I take you to one Kings game, you'll switch teams like *that*," he said, snapping his fingers.

Nose lifted, she responded, "Best of luck with that. I'd only go to a Kings' game if they were playing my Ducks!" With a cheeky beam, she raised her brows challengingly.

He nodded before using his green cotton jersey tank to wipe sweat off his forehead. She watched, noting his solid arms and dismissing the memory of his bicep contracting in her hand at work. "I'm here to talk business."

"Yes, of course you are," he said. They hiked toward a steeper, more difficult and less occupied trail. "My publicist's phone keeps ringing nonstop. Everyone's pissed *Slander* got an exclusive."

"Good. My boss loved it."

"So, shall we discuss the terms?"

"Of what?"

"You did me a solid, pulling that quote, *Barbie Blue*," he said, delivering that audacious wink. "I'd like to uphold my promise. And we are in public . . ."

She glared. Chase winked again and she shuddered, embarrassed for revealing her fantasy and at the notion of diddling a porn star, particularly the industry's sovereign ruler. "No sexual favors. I just need your help getting a few more stories, to free me from this wretched porn beat."

"Why are you so anti-porn?" he asked.

"Besides it being a seedy industry?"

"Aren't you a tabloid writer?"

"Point taken," she replied. "But celebrities know what they're getting into. Young girls entering porn don't."

Chase nodded. "Point taken."

"There's also STDs."

"We get tested every two weeks," he defended. "Anything else?"

She almost muttered *ruined relationships,* but refrained, simply sighing.

"You know," he continued, "most fans or reporters hang onto my every word."

"Well I'm happy to call bullshit on your asininities."

"No shit." His brows raised with intrigue. "So, why cover porn if you despise it?"

"Because my boss promised that afterward I could report on whatever I want, like *real* news."

"Porn is real. It's a billion-dollar industry."

Morgan huffed. "Please. There's no story or beauty. It's gonzo shots of girls basically getting raped." Their pace slowed as the hill steepened, but they were just beginning.

"It isn't rape!" he insisted. "It's consensual."

"Doesn't seem consensual half the time. Women are supposed to watch rough porn like that and explode?"

"Some women like hardcore scenes, Morgan."

"They're probably desensitized to violent porn with little else to turn to," she dismissed.

"Maybe for you civilians."

"Civilians?"

"What we porn players call you outsiders."

"Oh, are we a different species?"

Two teenage girls approached, pointing and whispering. Chase winked and they giggled. Morgan looked aside with contempt.

"Where were we?" he asked. "Right, violent porn. Look, I know some straight women watch lesbian porn because it's less vicious. But believe me, porn chicks thrive when it's rough and there's drama."

"That has to be a generalization."

"Not all, but many. Take my buddy. His angry porn star ex-girlfriend decided he cheated. One night she drives home, pulls into their garage and motors directly into him, crushing his pelvis against a wall so he can't use his dick anymore. These girls are psycho and violent."

Morgan saw a possible feature unfold, a profile of those violent men and women. "So male porn stars are angels?" she asked.

"We're just as messed up — former gangsters, drug dealers and punks. Not everyone. But male or female, we're mostly troubled outsiders who don't mesh elsewhere."

Morgan nodded as he continued.

"Tori was up there. Raised in a trailer park. Her sick perv uncle started touching her when she was four. When she turned fourteen, she fought back and he clobbered her. Violence was routine for Tor. We had some messy battles."

"You hit her?"

"Of course not," Chase reassured. "But fuck if I didn't punch a few walls in."

"What did you fight over?" Morgan asked.

He kept divulging, trusting Morgan even though she could publish any of it. "Dumb shit. Me texting female friends. Or

45

when I mentioned quitting performing to direct, she flipped her shit and pulled a knife."

Taken aback, Morgan's hand met her chest. "Seriously? You spent three years with someone that belligerent?"

Chase scratched behind his head. "Tor wanted me to go mainstream. I didn't care to cross over, but she pushed me to do *The E Word*."

The E Word was a widely publicized indie thriller film by an up-and-coming Hollywood director. When Chase scored a lead role two summers prior, everybody thought the Prince of Sin would be the first porn star to successfully cross into mainstream film. That was when he scored the Bradley Briefs ad campaign. But *The E Word* tanked at the box office. Mainstream media ridiculed Chase's failed attempt at *real* acting, before disregarding him.

"She needed to be this fake, tabloid-friendly couple," Chase revealed. "That's why I don't care what strangers think. It's all horseshit."

His laissez-faire image philosophy impressed Morgan. She'd been raised to present most respectably in a prim world. They hiked in silence for a moment until strangely, an out-of-site owl hooted. "You want to direct?"

"*Wanted*," he clarified, stiffening and scratching uncomfortably behind his neck. "But Tori's right, I know nothing about directing."

As they passed another group, one guy shouted, "Love your work, man!" Chase softened, high-fiving the guy. He took recognition in stride.

"And you?" Chase asked.

A raindrop skimmed her arm. "What about me?"

"Once you're *free from this wretched porn beat*, you'd like to work on *real* news?" When she simply shrugged, he asked, "What do you want to do with your life?"

"To make the news, not just report it," she explained,

breathing deeply as they approached the hilltop.

"How?"

"However I can," she responded, an enthused smile forming. "Perhaps I'll write world-changing features, do humanitarian work, bridge the gender gap, produce controversial films and market the fuck out of them, because all I do is read marketing blogs and brainstorm creative ways *Slander* could sell itself better."

They reached the summit to face hazy L.A. Catching her breath, Morgan clutched her ponytail in defeat. Inland, downtown skyscrapers vanished into darkening clouds. Westward, a continuous stream of airplanes landed at LAX, ushering more dreamers to the City of Angels. "How will I ever make a difference with twenty destinations and no GPS?"

To Chase, Morgan's response was sexier than anything he had heard in a long time. Almost daily, he met self-obsessed women counting Followers and Likes. But Morgan hoped to help others, to change the world for the better. Her compassion inspired awe.

He frowned, mortified at having once suggested a private session with someone so genuine. He'd never desired a woman's inner beauty, but suddenly nothing aroused him more. Marching over, he lifted her chin and softly kissed her. She closed her eyes, melting into his inviting lips.

When a raindrop splashed their noses, they separated and exchanged fraught glances. The sprinkle escalated, thunder erupting as people dashed to their cars. Chase and Morgan followed, carefully descending the summit under a thickening downpour. Reaching a plateau, Chase considered the view and saw that Grieta Profunda Canyon Park, the public hiking metropolis, was clearing out. He grabbed Morgan's hand. "Stop!"

She raised an eyebrow as he turned his hat backward before seizing her face. Their mouths met with force, tongues entwined, hearts racing. She bit that luscious lower lip, a craving finally fulfilled.

Besides a few ant-sized stragglers in the valley, they were completely alone. It was undeniably a public tryst, overlooking Los Angeles, yet sheets of rain placed them in safe seclusion.

Chase backed Morgan through bristly shrubs before pressing her against a steep slope. Dry dirt slopped into mud and splattered their legs, but neither cared, devouring each other their only concern.

He raised her tank top, tossed it aside and pecked down her neck. Moving his hands to her chest, he slipped two fingers beneath her sports bra, circling one taut nipple before kissing it lightly over the fabric. Lustfully she wailed, thrusting her chest toward his mouth.

Usually Chase preferred firm, fast fucks, particularly with new, casual flames. But he gladly teased Morgan, nibbling up her satin neck to a hungry mouth and embracing the change of pace.

Masterfully, he tugged her ponytail, commanding her head. He tilted it back to gnaw down her neck and chest. Reaching her stomach, he released her hair and crouched onto his knees. With delicate fingers, he slid her shorts down gradually, pecking along each bare leg. She stepped out of them as his tongue danced across her skin.

Morgan's breath deepened. Her eyes rolled back. He imagined filming her from each new angle, capturing her reactions to every unique touch.

"These don't work for me," he said gruffly, grasping her lingerie briefs with both hands and tearing the thin fabric. Using his teeth, he ripped them from her body.

She huffed incredulously as he tossed the ruined panties aside. "Fuck you," she barked. "Those are my favorite."

"Were your favorite," he corrected.

Morgan removed his baseball hat and casually tossed it into the mud. "Oops."

He shrugged. "You love this, you sleazy paparazzi."

"You're the sleaze ball, you seedy porn star," she rebutted, relishing each second. Usually Morgan rushed sex like an urgent deadline, but Chase left her hypnotized by each tantalizing, torturously slow kiss and touch. More than the rainstorm left her dripping wet.

Kneeled between her legs, Chase responded by licking circles around her belly button as his hands squeezed where thighs met toned behind. Exposed in just a bra, she evened the playing field by removing his tank top to reveal his coveted physique.

As his scruff tickled her thigh, she trembled. Morgan regretted leaving a landing strip at her last bikini wax, in case he preferred flawlessly bare performers. But concern dissipated as he finally kissed between her legs. Time to find out if those squealing orgasms he administered onscreen were real.

He slid two fingers inside her and placed his thumb over her swollen clit.

She had always wondered if porn stars really knew what they were doing. Now she knew. And she'd never forget. Moans escaped her mouth though panting breaths as he rubbed with a just-right pressure before gazing up with a cocksure leer.

"Still think porn stars are seedy?" he asked.

"Yes," she replied, staring into two smoldering, gold-tinted hazel eyes.

"Shame." Promptly removing his fingers, Chase grabbed his drenched tank top and stood.

"Don't stop," she griped.

"I won't hook up with a woman who considers me seedy." His voice sent tremors through her body as she ached for more tongue. "Fine," she complied with an irritated side-eye. "You aren't seedy."

Savoring the power he dangled, Chase asked, "What am I?"

"Spectacularly dexterous."

"What else?"

"I don't know," Morgan responded, shifting slightly. While she could assertively debate in work mode, dirty talk never came easily.

"Well, if you don't know . . ."

Watching him reach for his hat, worried the stirring adventure might end, she blurted, "You're a filthy sexpert."

He smiled appreciatively. "We can work on that." As she blushed, he tilted forward to kiss her.

To prevent him from stopping again, she yanked his shorts down, exposing soaked, tight black BB boxers that outlined a bulging erection. He leaned into her thigh, his tip grinding against her now throbbing clit.

"I need you inside me," she said with impressive candor. "Now."

As Chase found a condom in his wallet, Morgan side-eyed him. Though appreciative that he'd brought protection, she found it annoyingly presumptuous that he carried condoms everywhere.

"Stop with that immature side-eye," he demanded. "It's rude."

"Quit bossing me around," she responded.

Morgan grabbed the condom, kneeled, slid his briefs down and licked the tip of his rock-hard dick. While giving it a few sucks, she tore the condom wrapper. After placing the rubber on her lips, she hummed and slid it down his colossal shaft. Chase observed gratefully. Morgan hiccupped when his tip tickled behind her throat. He raised his brows.

"Mmmm," he responded, pulling out of her mouth,

helping her stand, and forcing her back against the mountain. Gently, he slid halfway inside her and she whimpered. Half of him had her feeling full.

"More, darling?" he asked.

"Mmm-hmm," she conceded.

"If it's too much, tell me to stop and I will," he promised.

She nodded, surprised by his considerateness. In his videos he showed no mercy. "Just do it already," she barked greedily.

He withdrew, spun her around and arched her body forward to enter from behind as they observed a blurred cityscape. His damp, deep breaths crashed against her ear like ocean waves, as though she were drowning in his furious sea.

"More," she insisted.

With Chase, women always craved more. And he always aimed to please. Determinedly, he gained force and speed before reaching around to rub her chest.

She roared. "Harder."

With Morgan's encouragement, he smacked against her behind unrelentingly and slid both hands along her feminine curves. He grabbed her waist to keep balance while circling her clit voraciously. Then he leaned close and whispered, "All of Los Angeles can see you."

At that, she climaxed, pelvic muscles clenching around his cock. Her shivering legs collapsed, but he steadied her hips. Quickly pumping to finish himself, he peaked with a growl, pinched her behind, and pulled out.

Morgan shifted nervously.

"Funny how you always wind up soaking wet around me," Chase commented lightly. Normally after a romp he wanted food, whiskey or sleep. Yet now, he wanted to stop time, to make the moment last.

"More hilarious is you thinking it's appropriate to destroy my favorite underwear."

"Sorry. Got caught up in the moment."

"Still, I expect you to replace those."

Suddenly, galloping footsteps stamped nearby. Morgan and Chase exchanged curious glances as the teenage girls from earlier giggled and sprinted past.

CHAPTER SEVEN: MR. BANANA PACKAGE

Chase jogged up the Culver City Stairs in Baldwin Hills, a low mountain range neighborhood overlooking Los Angeles from the south. When footsteps stamped behind him, he peered over his shoulder to Morgan a dozen steps below, jutting out her phone.

"A quote, Mr. Prince," she shouted. "Give me a story!"

He sped up, skipping stairs. She followed.

"Mr. Prince!"

Jumping three, four, five steps at once, he leaped but never approached the mountaintop.

"I need one quote!" Morgan growled, grasping his leg as he tumbled toward a cold, cruddy ground.

Chase jolted awake, forehead coated in sweat. He caught his breath observing Cleo asleep beside him. Earlier that night, Morgan had texted, asking if they could meet again, strictly for business. He appreciated her persistence but doubted either of them could maintain strictly professional relations. So he'd ghosted her, certain Morgan was feisty enough to score a porn exposé without his assistance.

Half an hour later, he tossed in bed, fixated on her. But instead of picturing her pert ass slapping his groin, he imagined future Morgan shooting a prizewinning documentary someplace exotic. Depressingly, he figured he'd still be rotting this shady apartment complex, jerking off to his spank bank highlight reel.

Despite a scheduled session with his bodybuilding coach

later, Chase resolved to vanquish thoughts of Morgan Sidney by sweating her out. The Prince of Sin's notorious abs weren't carved from one-a-days.

As he slipped out of bed, Cleo woke and trailed him. Her collar jangled as he clanged into furniture, searching for workout gear. After getting dressed and leashing Cleo, he bolted out into darkness, toward a far-off, lit-up Santa Monica pier. The black sky warmed to indigo then shades of yellow and orange. But the Venice boardwalk remained considerably deserted. Bicycle chains reeled as two cyclists passed. Up ahead, a homeless man murmured about the Lord. As Chase jogged further, the only sounds were his and Cleo's footsteps and the Pacific Ocean rippling at low tide.

Chase's busy mind superseded the tranquility, wondering if he should text his persistent associate to arrange another meeting. He owed Morgan two more fantasies but preferred keeping liaisons with non-girlfriends "one and done." And he never dated civilians, especially not reporters who adeptly encouraged personal divulgence.

Reaching a pier-side gymnasium, he grabbed a pull up bar, committed to pulling Morgan from memory. As sunlight emerged, he hoisted up and down, clenching mighty arms, strapping shoulders and a sturdy back. A diehard fanbase motivated him — women worldwide, perhaps even Morgan, touching themselves while fantasizing about his rippling muscles.

Jumping down to rest against a cement wall, he drew his phone and searched Morgan Sidney online. The first link featured a list of her *Slander* stories, like *How to rock a lob* and *The official ranking — What determines a celeb's A, B, C or D-list status.* His stomach sank while scanning such hollow reportage.

A clump of bird crap plopped onto the cement beside his pristine gray mesh sneakers. Above, a lone seagull squawked. She soared freely, the way Chase wished Morgan could.

Fortunately, he stood in a unique position to rescue Morgan from vlogging about hairdos and socialites. And perhaps, he surmised, while being so graciously facilitative, he might score some action of appreciation. Scrolling through his contacts, he found Morgan's name.

Dressed in denim shorts, a side cut tank top and gold-rimmed black aviators, Morgan waited patiently near Muscle Beach Venice. In Venice, bohemian was trendy, so she blended right in wearing a fringe leather satchel, half-up braid and vintage roller skates. Stretched against a railing, she watched two topless beefy orange dudes in spandex spot each other while lifting weights. One glanced over and flexed a bicep. She shook her head, turned away and crossed her arms.

Since Chase had suggested a hike, Morgan chose their next excursion. She selected the boardwalk to observe him in his newfound neighborhood. This time, she was determined to find Jason's feature story and liberate herself without succumbing to Chase's charms.

Typical weekend crowds jammed the promenade. Lively music played as street dancers rocked impressive acrobatics. Besides never-ending tourist clusters, Venice Beach promised epic people-watching as a hub for stoners, skater kids and modern-day hippies who lived and let live.

The Prince of Sin emerged distinctly, wheeling over on a longboard with Cleo in tow. "Darling," he announced, arms opening. But she crouched and met the pooch, leaving Chase mid-air hug. He cleared his throat enviously.

Morgan assessed his wheels. "Nice longboard."

"I have a longer one." And then that signature wink.

Side-eying him, she returned to the doggy. "Who's this little guy?"

"*She*," Chase corrected, "is Cleopatra."

"Because you appreciate finer things?" she retorted,

standing to meet him.

"Because I appreciate strong, driven women." His eyes tracked her figure.

"*Smooooooth*," she cooed. "But I refuse to be enchanted."

Together they skated the walkway, scanning souvenir shops and compelling artisan booths while dancers and musicians performed. Chase stopped when his phone rang, so she skated to an art stall.

"Yup," Chase said, rejoining Morgan. "I'll be ready. Thanks, Benny." He clicked off and noticed her entranced by a sunflower painting. Discreetly, he snapped several candid photos before rejoining her.

"Sunflowers are my favorite," she explained. "Was that Benny Solomon?"

"Someone's done their homework," Chase responded as they continued along the boardwalk.

"Great journalists get the story no matter what. Even after Benny's assistant hung up on me when I first attempted to track you down."

Chase chuckled. "At least somebody in that office has my back. Benny just explained that they messed up my Friday flight again."

"Where to?"

"New York."

"Shooting a few N.Y.C. special features?" she asked. "Taxi Drive-her? Breakfast *in* Tiffany?" Morgan grinned.

He chuckled. "You're funny. You should produce."

"Now you're the funny one. I'm anti-porn."

Chase knew many civilians challenged pornography but wondered why Morgan despised it so vehemently. "Actually," he explained. "I'm shooting banana holder ads for a Japanese company."

"Banana holders?"

"*Real* bananas. These banana-shaped containers that keep

the fruit from getting squished in your bag."

Her chocolatey brown eyes squinted as she laughed boisterously. "What?" she asked. "Why are you promoting that?"

"Apparently, I'm big in Japan."

"More than the sun must be rising over there."

"What?" he asked with a confused smirk.

"Japan. Land of the Rising Sun. Rising . . . Never mind.
Why do you accept such silly gigs?"

"You think I reel in dough from porn?" he asked.

Morgan shrugged, presuming.

"The real money's in sponsorship. Which is why I'm proud
to be Mr. Banana Package or whatever."

She typed *Sponsorship* into her phone notes before wheeling to catch up with Chase.

"Enough about my ridiculous side hustles," he continued.
"Tell me what our next sexcapade will be."

"Excuse me, but that is not happening again." Blushing,
she avoided eye contact.

"Course it is, darling. I owe you two more fantasies. Tell
me your next."

"Let's get ice cream," she said, skating to a soft serve shop.
They ordered chocolate-vanilla swirl cones and both reached
for their wallets.

"On me," he offered, pulling out cash.

"I prefer paying my share," Morgan responded, handing
three dollar bills to a pimply, teenage cashier.

Chase nodded and split his money. The girl giggled as she
took the cash. He winked before they skated away.

"Most men insist on paying," Morgan noted.

"You said you prefer paying," Chase responded. "I won't
fight my date's preference."

"Do you mean this stuff or are you just trying to score
again?"

"I'm just being me," he said in earnest.

She nodded, considering the move surprisingly gentlemanly. "This isn't a date."

They sat on a giant cement block and admired the sunset. Chase licked his ice cream seductively, tongue writhing. Meeting his challenge, Morgan moistened her lips, leaned close and pressed her tongue to his cone. He dragged his tongue along the cool dessert, grazing her velvety lips, and paused. Their warm breaths tangled like the chocolate-vanilla swirl.

"Tell me what you'd like me to do with you," he whispered, searching her sweet bronzed eyes. When she didn't respond, he bent for a kiss, but she cautiously withdrew.

Face scrunched, she shook her head and deflected, "What would you want?"

"Easy," he said, lying down. His shirt rose, revealing hunky abs. "I want to be bossed around."

"For real?" she asked. He never took submissive roles online, so this surprised her. Morgan gazed at his waistband, her front tooth chewing into her lower lip.

"My exes, all industry girls, enjoyed receiving spankings and getting called whores."

Morgan gulped at the word *whore* and shut her eyes.

Chase continued, "They needed to be dominated. For me to have my way with them. It'd be nice to relinquish control for once."

She opened her eyes to his heartfelt expression. Sunlight illuminated his jade eyes, making one appear darker than the other. Morgan inched closer to examine them, but he popped up.

"It's easy to talk about this stuff," he said.

"Well, it's your *job*."

"Why can't you discuss sex?"

Morgan's gaze meandered toward the sea. She inhaled deeply, tasting a salty sea breeze, and tugged her gold bangle bracelet. "My mom is more traditional. She taught me to wait until marriage to . . . make whoopee. Then I started high school and learned there were other options. But I couldn't discuss those options with my conservative mother or reserved little sister. I had to teach myself, through magazines, TV and awkward first times."

"What about your dad?" His arm cradled her waist in a compassionate side hug.

She leaned on his shoulder for a nanosecond, then edged from his grasp and pulled up her phone notepad. After clearing her throat, she asked, "What's your family like?"

Dejected, he bowed his head. "It's just me and Ma," he explained. "Always has been. She taught me that sex was normal and natural, never swept it under any rugs. When I was seven, she took me to an art class where she modeled nude. We were one of *those* households." He shook his head, remembering, then asked, "Wouldn't your ex-boyfriends help you explore your desires?"

Swallowing, she stared down, looking like a child as she kicked her roller-skates.

"Never mind," he said, running his fingers over her manicured nails before clasping her hand. "I won't push."

Morgan's gaze lifted and they locked eyes—his considerate, hers narrowing. "You can push me later. What I need is a porn exposé."

Chase grinned and stood. "Better idea," he said. "I challenge you to a race. *When* I win, you disclose your second fantasy. If by some miracle you triumph, I'll assist with your story."

"Good luck." Morgan's almond-colored eyes burned into his sly, forest-green ones. "You'll need it."

Several blocks from Venice's main drag, Chase and Morgan stood feet apart on a quiet residential side street. "First one around that pothole and back here wins," Chase instructed, pointing to a street pole he'd tied Cleo's leash to. The dog paced back and forth, eyeing them.

"On three," she declared. Taking position, she counted and they jetted off.

Chase sped ahead, Morgan close behind. Cleo barked furiously. As Chase rounded the pothole, his longboard hit a gaping crack and wheeled out from underneath him. Morgan grinned, spinning around him and racing ahead.

But he jumped back on and surged forward full force. Cleo woofed fiercely, tugging on her leash. Just as Chase caught up, Cleo broke free and sprinted toward them. He tried wheeling around her but fell as she jumped up.

"Yes!" Morgan shouted victoriously, grabbing the street post. She skated to where he lay on the street with Cleo licking his face. Bending down to tousle Cleo's fur, she pulled a water bottle from her satchel and chugged.

Grinning smug as ever, he announced, "Winner winner, chicken dinner."

"Nice try," she objected.

"I said first to Cleo wins!"

"You pointed to that pole," she corrected. "So I guess you're assisting with my feature, Your Highness." She extended an arm to help him up.

"Guess so, darling," he said. "Come to set tomorrow. You'll meet everyone and get the real story."

"Wow!" Morgan responded, stoked and hoping it would lead to the end. She took another sip of water. "What's tomorrow's shoot?"

"A ten-on-one interracial gangbang."

Eyes bulging, she wheezed, spewing water everywhere.

CHAPTER EIGHT: THE GANGBANG

Morgan parked in an overpriced downtown lot and walked several blocks to the address Chase had texted. There she found a construction site—a literal hole in the ground. Around her, business as usual befell hasty, muggy Downtown Los Angeles. Businessmen in slim-fit suits dashed past homeless people driving shopping carts of knickknacks. Rocker teens cut class to smoke joints on a bench. A young woman in a pencil skirt scurried by balancing two trays of Starbucks cups. The city abuzz, there were no gangbangs to be seen.

I think I'm lost, she texted Chase. Moments later, he shouted her name from a gated entrance to what appeared to be a hardware store. Hurrying over, she asked, "Did I have the wrong address?"

"We give out a fake," Chase explained. "So the safety board can't come sniffing around. They used to be crazy strict enforcing condom rules."

Morgan jotted *Condoms rules* into a paper notebook as Chase opened a locked gate.

For a decade, Jimmy Druck shot porn exclusively for Clay's Empire at the company's massive headquarters in the Northwest Valley. The splashy building held studios and sets for any scene imaginable. In its heyday, when more people actually paid for porn, the compound boomed with activity. But as streaming dominated and work at Clay's Empire slowed, Jimmy drained his savings to purchase his own production studio downtown. Now he freelanced, still shooting for Lit

Empire Entertainment but also other industry bigwigs.

"Jimmy's fine to have you here," Chase explained. "But no photos or filming."

Nodding, Morgan followed him into a tight, organized office. Signed pinup girl posters adorned the wall behind a giant, mahogany desk. At a smaller metal desk, Bob edited footage on a monitor. He glanced up as they entered.

"Bob-o!" Chase yelped excitedly, patting Bob's robust back. "Remember Morgan?" Bob glanced up, face tight. "She's cool, she's with me." Mumbling, Bob returned his gaze to the screen. "Bob's the Salt to Jimmy's Pepper," Chase explained. "The gin to his tonic."

Chase led Morgan down a narrow corridor to a bright makeup den where a short, plump woman with round cheeks aligned brushes on a counter. Morgan tried to place her.

"Carly, meet Morgan. She's exposing porn for *Slander*."

"*Covering* porn," Morgan corrected.

"Hi!" Carly waved sweetly.

"She's our stylist," Chase explained giddily, thrilled to have Morgan at work. As they continued down a hallway, he whispered, "You know who that was?"

Morgan gave a stumped shrug.

"Creemy Carly!"

"No way!" She glanced back toward the makeup room. A decade earlier, every guy at Morgan's high school wanted a piece of Creemy Carly. "She's a stylist now? Does she still perform?"

"Nope. Married and raising, like, five kids. A total sweetheart. We've had some *good* times."

Morgan abstained from pressing for details but scribbled *Life after porn* in her notes.

Chase toured Morgan around the open-concept studio's various sections, which included stage, gym, bedroom and street sets. Unlike the sketchy warehouse she'd visited last time, Jimmy's place was glossily lit, with ceilings several stories high. It smelled like fresh cleaning products and had character, its brick interior walls painted with an original hardware store logo from the 1950s.

"Boys, meet Morgan!" Chase announced as they entered the bedroom stage area. A group of guys chilled out, listening to '90s rap. Several of them glanced, others remained fixed to their phones. "She's covering our industry and, well, me for *Slander*, so be sure to embellish my amazingness." Some guys laughed with Chase, who winked at Morgan before sauntering to a bathroom.

These were the stereotypical porn dudes she anticipated: beefy, crude, tattoos. Before Chase, she'd have assumed they were all dirty thugs, but then, he hadn't been all she expected.

As she sat on the bed corner, guys approached to check her out, flirt and inquire what her deal was. "What exactly you writin' 'bout?" asked a black performer with tired eyes and a goatee.

"Not sure yet," Morgan admitted. "I'm playing with life after porn, condom laws . . . I've been shadowing Chase to explore the porn world for ideas."

"Prince ain't your average porn brah, baby," he explained, nodding to one of the guys. "My buddy there, Rock, has connections to the Crips. We don't ask what connections, but you don't wanna piss him off. And Freddie's got like four kids from four different mamas. These brahs are your porno norm."

"Like you?" she asked, scribbling notes.

"Nahh," he said, waving a hand and emitting a whiff of his spicy, woodsy body spray. "I ain't important. But for your story, know that white guys in porn get more chances. It's a grind for everybody, but there's less work for brothers. And when directors do go black, most stick with well-known guys. It's a *hard* gig, pun intended." Hollering, he revealed several gold teeth. "We got into porn to make quick, easy cash, but it ain't quick or easy. And it's no simpler for my wife." He tapped a platinum band on his ring finger. "She's a black performer, too."

Morgan jotted *Race* as he transitioned into the staying-power struggles female porn stars faced. With so many worthy discourses to explore, it seemed unfortunate that Jason would likely prefer she disclose something superficial, like the prevalence of ass implants. Morgan didn't care to spill the tea on which smut stars secretly sported silicone.

"What's your name?" Morgan asked.

"Tiger Trece, baby," he said, extending a hand. A metal tooth glinted through a shifty grin. "Trece, as in the number of inches I've got." Again, he hollered.

"Thirteen?" She shook his hand but tilted her head doubtfully. "I'm Morgan Sidney."

Across the studio, Chase helped Jimmy and Bob set up. Bob positioned lights on the street stage and fixed a green screen nearby. Chase cleaned Jimmy's camera lens.

"Lads, show Kali your tests before we start!" Jimmy shouted.

"Show me IDs," Bob added, enforcing the porn method to ensure nobody was underage.

"Let's have a chinwag," Jimmy said to Chase, slapping his back. "I got more gen on Viola Emperor. She only lets Tori shoot girl-girl now." He paused, trying to evaluate Chase's glazed reaction, then continued, "No shocker there. Viola doesn't want a man poking Tori with his John Thomas when she can't. Viola's one dodgy lady."

It wasn't astounding that Viola controlled Chase's ex. Often when a porn girl hooked a new boyfriend, or girlfriend in Tori's case, she suddenly wouldn't book anal, or boy-girl, or any whatever-her-new-beau-opposed scenes. Eventually that girl resented her lover and the relationship ended in bloody, furniture flinging turmoil. What was shocking was how few fucks Chase gave hearing Tori's name, a post-breakup first. Glancing at Morgan taking interest in his life, he considered making her his.

"Got your scepter, boyo?" Jimmy asked.

"Oh." Chase scratched behind his head. "I'm . . . still not using that thing."

Jimmy furrowed his brows but didn't argue. He had witnessed countless melodramatic porn splits. Usually performers found freedom after escaping a turbulent relationship, but Chase remained stuck. Moving on, Jimmy turned to Bob. "Start with BTS," he instructed. "Kali, love, you ready for behind-the-scenes?"

"*Sì,*" Kali Sensuale rasped, her throaty smoker's voice stirring the room. A voluptuous Italian beauty entered, costumed in a sparkly purple bikini and come-fuck-me heels that boosted her from five-foot-one to an easy five-foot-six. She had smooth light-brown skin and long glossy dark hair. An enchantress with dark upturned eyes, Kali flaunted sensual curves and an exceptionally large, all-natural chest.

After half a decade in the game, Kali felt at ease despite bracing to take it in all three holes from eleven well-endowed men. Eleven, because Jimmy booked one extra for his "Ten Man Interracial Gangbang with Anal," in case of a no-show. Bob in tow, Kali strutted to the bathroom for a pre-shoot enema. Passing the bedroom set, she noticed Morgan chatting up the guys. "Who is the civilian?" she asked Jimmy and Chase.

"Just my friend," Chase told Kali.

"*Bambino,* with you, they are never *solo un'amica.*" Kali's exotic eyes glared. Before Tori, Chase had let tons of bimbos come and go. Kali sauntered to the bathroom. Bob followed with a camera and slammed the door.

Since shooting their first scene together four years prior,

Kali and Chase had become close friends. At the time, she took night classes toward a bachelor's degree in human sexuality. Despite being six years younger than Chase, Kali saw him as a baby brother. He always curiously pestered her about essay topics or lectures, even more so once she began researching her master's thesis.

Kali's scholastic endeavors were admirable, but her professional prowess was awe-inspiring. She experienced sexual pleasure in a deeper, more elevated manner than most. Kali could make any scene seem real. Playing a school girl, the twenty-four-year-old became barely-legal, with huge optimistic eyes and that know-it-all confidence of youth. As a dominatrix, she barked orders and cracked a whip to instill terror. Her full being engaged — mind, body and soul.

Once Bob and Kali finished in the bathroom, Jimmy organized the guys. He distributed tacky gear like baseball hats, beanies and shirts, all branded with Lit Empire's logo, before outlining their scene.

Morgan watched from the bed, twirling her bangle bracelet apprehensively. But from accessories to storyline, the tackiness helped her chill. Bob played '80s rock music and the group did a run-through as Jimmy captured still shots. Kali strutted out the back door of a "nightclub" and onto the street set. The eleven guys quickly cornered her, stripping her slowly when she couldn't repay a debt. As Jimmy's camera clicked and flashed, a few guys slapped and jiggled Kali's ass.

Morgan inhaled deeply. As Kali stripped, the men whipped out their dicks, each longer or fatter than the last. Morgan's eyes bulged catching a glimpse of Tiger Trece's at least foot-long hog.

Finally naked, Kali fell to her knees and moaned swallowing each cock. Jimmy ordered his squad to keep the ball rolling, so soon enough they entered her pussy consecutively, each posing for Jimmy's still camera. Next, they double penetrated Kali, vaginally and anally.

Morgan's ex had been into gangbang scenes, and occasionally she'd grown wet watching with him, but nothing about this performance stimulated her. It seemed orderly, businesslike. Until the moment Chase Prince entered Kali Sensuale, eliciting deep jealousy and whirring anger within Morgan. Each jabbing thrust and moan exhaled tempted her to rip them apart. But he wasn't her man, so why did she long to punch Kali's desirous, enraptured grin?

"More rough," Kali insisted. "Give it to me."

Flashes flickered as Chase spanked her jiggly ass. "Whore," he asserted.

Morgan's eyelids tightened, the word triggering haunting flashbacks. As Chase's waist slapped Kali, she pinched her lips and attempted inhaling to a slow count of three. Instead, her chest tightened and her face flushed. She sauntered to the bathroom.

Clutching the ceramic pedestal sink, she scrutinized her reflection in the mirror. Wavy brown tendrils adhered to her damp forehead. Her skin faded gray in the florescent lighting. She gagged a chunk of egg whites into the sink and caught her breath.

Eventually, she pinched her lips, inhaled to a slow count of three, then exhaled to a slow count of six. *"Great journalists immerse themselves in any subject,"* she reminded herself with another breath in — one, two, three. *"Despite their interests or fears, they take risks to get the story no matter what."* She exhaled smoothly — one, two, three, four, five, six. Color reluctantly returned to her face.

After rinsing her mouth, she returned to the bed and continued observing the animalistic sex scene. When guys weren't in Kali, they meandered, rubbing their cocks, occasionally strolling past Morgan to grab antibacterial wipes. Some stopped to ask her questions or simply give her flirtatious eyes.

"Get it together, mates!" Jimmy shouted, more like a summer camp counselor to preteens than a film director. "Even if you aren't inside Kali, stay in my bloody shot, behind whoever is. And keep watching the sex!" Changing a camera setting, he mumbled, "I hate bloody gangbangs." Scenes with fewer performers were simpler.

After shooting stills, they took a break before resuming filming. Eleven husky, nude men roamed unperturbed. For them, it was just another day at the office. Morgan cupped behind her head and leisurely leaned against the wall. Anything could feel natural if those around you normalized it.

Chase plopped beside her in black BBs. "Where'd you disappear to before?"

"Just needed air."

Jimmy approached and asked, "Care to do a walk-on?"

"What?" Morgan asked, confused.

"A hundred bucks to do a cameo," Jimmy offered. "You can leave the club with Kali and take off when the guys show up. We can even give you a porn name in the credits. Up to you, love." Then he waltzed to the kitchen breezily, as though he'd offered her a stick of gum.

This was a serious invitation, one industry-loathing Morgan seriously considered. A porno cameo could reroute someone's destiny if a future employer or loved ones found out. Plus it could be a slippery slope—first, one assumes fully-clothed, walk-on roles, next their top's coming off, and then . . .

"Ignore him," Chase said, fists tight. It was unlike Jimmy to make such an offer without consulting him first.

"YOLO," she said.

"Pardon?"

"Great journalists take risks," she explained. "Maybe I can't embrace erotica until fully embodying it."

"Morgan," Chase placed a hand on her leg.

She edged from his grasp. After all, he'd just fucked another woman. "When will I have this opportunity again?" Smile aglow, she sprung up. "I kind of want to do it."

"Kind of?" Chase asked.

"Not kind of. I want to!"

"What about your family?" he asked.

She shrugged. "I can't forfeit opportunities because of other people's potential reactions." That was Mandi's method, not hers. "Don't worry, I'll keep my clothes on."

"You sure?" Chase questioned, rubbing behind his head.

"Positive. I'm stoked!" Mostly, she was.

Clad in a bandage pleather miniskirt, crop halter top and towering platform sandals, Barbie Blue exited Club XXX alongside Kali Sensuale. When a group of provoking men approached, Barbie Blue darted off.

"Cut!" Jimmy shouted.

Morgan erupted laughing, her acting debut a success. Though not Oscar-worthy, the performance received high praise. Guys high-fived her and Jimmy extended a fist bump before extending a crumpled hundred-dollar bill.

"Considering a career one-eighty?" Chase asked, examining her endless legs. Silently, he prayed she wouldn't seriously consider his line of work.

Morgan raised both brows with a sly smirk and shoulder shrug before turning on her heels toward the restroom. Her cheeky bottom poking out underneath such a skimpy miniskirt gave him a semi.

After she'd changed back into everyday attire, Morgan returned to the bed as Jimmy started filming. The sequence began as before, but instead of classic rock blasting and a camera's flash, the performers acted, if you could call it that. Morgan stifled laughs as Chase demanded Kali settle up.

Kali shimmied and shook as everyone hollered. She stripped seductively, revealing her groomed bush with a landing strip not unlike Morgan's. Rubbing her tits and clit as the guys penetrated interchangeably, Kali wailed and begged and fluttered her eyes. A hazy line separated her from the indebted Call Girl, as though she wasn't performing at all.

Again, the guys roamed disinterestedly when it wasn't their turn. Sweaty and exhausted, they jerked themselves to remain semi-hard. Only Chase's wood stood bewitchingly erect without him ever touching it.

"Grab some lube." Jimmy grunted, glancing around. "Bob!"

With Bob missing, Chase stepped in, grabbing a jar of coconut oil from the supply table beside Morgan. He passed it to the guys, who smeared it onto their cocks.

"Coconut oil?" Morgan asked.

"It's the best lubricant," Chase whispered, winking and adding, "You'll see." She shuddered with both anticipation and revulsion at another round with him.

Suddenly, a light sizzled and abruptly blew out. "Bob!" Jimmy screamed. Chase charged, following the cord to a nearby plug. He disconnected the cable, switched to a different outlet and returned to set in seconds, ready to go.

After nearly another hour of filming, everyone's energy dipped. The other guys lazed, sweaty and sunken, but Chase remained impressively tactful, hopping around to assist Jimmy.

"Focus, guys! Fuck, man!" Jimmy shouted. "Take five. Start envisioning pops."

Kali approached Morgan with clammy hair and smudged makeup. She grabbed a body wipe. "There's mascara in my holes," she told Morgan woozily, giggling and scrubbing between her legs. Leering, she met Morgan's gaze and added, "But I love it."

"Where in bloody hell is that man?" Jimmy shouted. "Bob!" Finally, Bob sauntered in. "Ah, he lives! Order a few pizzas, mate." Bob grunted and left. "Food's on its way. Let's finish with A-T-Ms, then pops."

"A-T-Ms?" Morgan asked Kali, who ignored her and returned to set.

"And it's not over when you're done," Jimmy continued. "No running to take a piss, no wipes. Stay on set and in my shot. We're not done until the last guy pops. And I need more fucking energy, lads."

"Do it for me," Kali chimed in her sexy accent. Like a coach before the team's final play, she instructed, "Be aggressive. I go back to Italy tomorrow. Give me what to remember."

Ever a team captain, Chase sprang into determined action. "If we stand here and move in like so . . ." he instructed. Everybody nodded to his demonstration of the best angles for Jimmy's shot.

Jimmy called action and Tiger stepped forward, pumping into Kali's asshole as she lay on a bench, legs lifted. Then he flipped her upward and slid his member into her mouth. Kali's pep talk and Chase's guidance worked. One by one, they animatedly followed suit. Ass to mouth, A-T-M.

Closing the sequence with several loud grunts, Chase grinded his dick inside Kali's mouth. "Look at me, bitch," he ordered, and their gazes locked.

Watching Chase nail another woman no longer instilled Morgan's green envy. After he'd kicked ass leading the pack all day, she respected him more. He was the type of champion she needed on her arm. But could she make him hers?

The scene concluded with Kali kneeled, welcoming eleven consecutive, sloppy face shots. Bob carried in fresh pizzas as Jimmy captured post-explosion still-camera shots of Kali mid circle jerk while semen drizzled down her damp body. Eventually he called, "Cut."

The men hurried to the bathroom or grabbed wipes to clean off. But naked, cum-coated Kali Sensuale paraded straight toward the pizzas, ripped a slice and chomped an enormous, gooey bite. Standing bare before Morgan, she snacked voraciously as the semen of eleven men seeped into her pores. Thankfully, pungent pepperoni masked soggy spunk.

"Nice legs, civilian," Kali said, appraising Morgan while gnawing another chunk.

"Thanks?" Morgan answered.

Kali devoured the slice without another word and sashayed away. As she left, the guys flocked for food, some naked, others not. Morgan waited until the performers were fed before grabbing a piece and searching for Chase. Spotting him freshly showered, clothed and bench pressing in the gym, she approached.

"Mind blown, darling?"

Refusing him bragging rights, she cleared her throat. "Well for starters, no wonder women fake orgasms. Kali just simulated, like, seventeen."

"Maybe she wasn't simulating."

"Even if they were genuine, this is the standard boys and men hold average women to."

Chase responded with a huff, pressing the barbell. "Yeah, seventeen is a lot. Even my pussy-pleasing record is only twelve in a row."

"Only," she mocked, side eyeing. "And you must have taken a little blue pill."

Shaking his head, he adjusted on the bench, leaning in to whisper, "Negative. But most of these bums do. Darling, I'm a pro." He bit into her pizza and returned to doing chest presses.

"You were fine," Morgan said, refusing to christen him porn's great one. "But Kali stole the show. After performing my own brief cameo, I can understand her fervor. It's juicily scintillating to have all eyes on you." She licked her lips and teased, "Maybe I should consider a career one-eighty."

Jaw tight, Chase lost his grip, dropping the weight to its rack.

Beers got tossed around. Chase took two and offered one to Morgan, who shook her head. "Tempting as it is to party the day away with fucking's finest, I should get going." Grabbing her bag, she thanked Jimmy, Bob and the guys before Chase walked her out.

"You think you know nothing about directing, but you were unbelievable today," she encouraged. "No doubt you could direct, if you really focused on your craft." She nodded to his beer, adding, "And maybe cut back on partying."

"Thanks," he said before pecking her forehead. Only his mom had ever suggested he could achieve anything besides ejaculation. "See you when I'm back in town?"

"Perhaps," she responded, stepping into the downtown twilight. "If I still require your expertise."

After locking the gate, he spun around to Kali Sensuale's watchful eyes peering over a gender studies textbook, her body and hair twined by towels. "Bambino, you are in trouble."

A headshake and mocking expression illustrated his disagreement. To avoid Kali's probing, he ripped the towel from her head and sprinted away. She dropped her textbook and gave chase.

CHAPTER NINE: CENTER ICE

Chase didn't reach out to Morgan while he was in New York. No texts, snaps, calls, Instas, no sliding into her DMs . . . So when Grant Wexler invited her to a hockey game, she accepted.

The night arrived and Morgan opened her apartment door to Prince Charming. Fetching and tall with piercing blue eyes, Grant Wexler was clean shaven with side-parted light blond hair and a trim, athletic build. Dapper in a wool and cashmere sport coat, cotton trousers and leather shoes, he carried an extravagant white rose and French peony bouquet.

"Good evening," he said, beaming a toothy smile and handing her the flowers. "May I come inside?"

She smirked. With Chase, there would be some quip or inuendo there. But Morgan waved Grant in and turned to locate the ceramic vase she'd purchased at a Tel Aviv market.

"You look adorable," Grant bellowed. Her vintage Mighty Ducks jersey clashed with his rakish vibe. "Though you're rooting for the wrong team."

Like Chase, Grant was an L.A. Kings fan. Except Chase hadn't invited her to this specific game—Ducks at Kings, their rivalry matchup. She wondered if he was still in New York, then forced away unwanted distractions and listened as Grant detailed the venture capitalist world. Their forced and formal chitchat reminded her of polite conversations with strangers. But Grant proved polite and smart, traits that would tick off a checklist if she had one, so she gave him a chance.

After opening the front door, Grant followed her to his Tesla Model X, where he again held the door open. Unaccustomed to such chivalry, she stiffened.

"All good?" Grant asked.

Morgan nodded as he started the car and they jetted down the street.

Seconds later, Chase Prince's motorcycle thundered, hugging a corner and speeding up Morgan's block.

"Beers on me," Morgan said, rifling through her wallet.

"Don't you dare," Grant insisted, emitting a hearty chuckle and placing his exclusive credit card directly into the cashier's hand. "I would never let my date pay."

Morgan extended her card. "No, I insist. These tickets were already on you."

"They're company seats. And *I* insist," he reiterated.

Withdrawing, she gave an irritated side-eye, then smirked, remembering how Chase resented that habit.

"I'm a gentleman," Grant explained.

"Do you ever wonder if it's more gentlemanly to go Dutch, if it's what your date prefers?"

"Can't I be debonair without being sexist?" Grant rebutted, slightly harshly.

Huffing it off, she recalled splitting the ice cream tab with Chase at the beach, those three bucks speaking volumes.

They carried foamy beers to Grant's firm's front-row center ice seats. "To the honor of finally meeting you," he said. They tapped plastic cups. "I must say, you're prettier than your sister described. And tougher to secure a date with."

"The life of a working woman," Morgan responded, admiring an undisturbed view of the buzzing Staples Center. Sweat dripped down the Ducks' captain's face as he warmed up.

"You write for *Slander*, correct?" Grant asked.

"I write, I vlog, I squander my soul."

"So you're a wordsmith, an artist. Discovering different ways to sell my partners on riskier investments is how I get creative. And if they won't budge, I invest on my own," he said, winking a sky-blue eye.

Her lips thinned into a fake, closed-mouthed smile. His wink lacked the Prince of Sin's *cool* factor.

"As long as you love what you do," he continued. "My strategy for choosing any venture has more to do with a team's passion than their experience."

Morgan respected Grant's tact. If only she possessed that level of passion for vlogging.

"Care for my blazer?" he offered once the game commenced.

"I'm all right." She slipped into her leather coat. Morgan prided herself for being smart enough to bring her own jacket. But Grant was simply being polite, so she thanked him.

As they chatted, the conversation always circled back to him. When she mentioned undergraduate studies in the Midwest, he boasted about his MBA. Her dad having interviewed four of the past five Presidents shifted to Grant once shaking then-Senator Obama's hand.

Tied one-all, the game ripened while the date remained stale, at least for Morgan. Until halfway through the second period, when a classic love song played and the kiss cam popped onscreen. Considering Grant's ostentatious style, Morgan immediately predicted they'd be planned prey. When they appeared onscreen, she pecked her jaunty date's cheek. But Grant grasped Morgan's cheeks and swooped in for a smooch.

Chase accidentally dropped his hot dog into the man in front's sweatshirt hood. "Bambino?" Kali asked, seated beside Chase in the rowdy upper bowl. Following his eyes to the jumbotron, she glimpsed Morgan's kiss before it switched to an adorable elderly couple. Kali frowned, carefully removing the hot dog before the guy noticed.

But Chase didn't process Kali's words, ketchup stains on his white sneakers, or everybody going berserk when the Kings' goalie made a huge save. Instead, he tapped his foot agitatedly and eventually muttered, "Whatever. Just another civilian."

Kali placed a protective hand on his heart. After the second period, with the Kings down three to one, Chase felt more scorned by Morgan than the score. For the first time ever, he left a Kings game before the final buzzer.

Morgan delighted in high spirits after a four to two Ducks win. Additionally, she hoped going out with Grant would get Mandi off her back. He wasn't Mr. Right, but he also wasn't a bad guy, and at least she'd given him a chance.

Walking to her apartment door, she and Grant spotted a bouquet of sunflowers and small black box on the mat. Certain Chase had come by, she beamed, relieved he hadn't forgotten their connection.

Off Morgan's enthusiasm, Grant stepped back decidedly. "My apologies if I rambled tonight," he said, running a shaky hand through his quaffed hair. "I know I can be over the top, opening doors and all that jazz. But I was raised a gentleman and believe a lady deserves so. Chivalry only dies if we kill it."

"Thanks for a great night," she said. "Let's stay in touch."

"Certainly," he responded with a head bow before proceeding downstairs.

Morgan snagged the gifts and scurried inside to replace Grant's elaborate bouquet with Chase's sunflowers. Then she opened the tiny, cardboard gift box to a pair of Ducks boy briefs, like the pair he'd destroyed on their hike rendezvous.

She'd never sent a racy photo. But tonight she craved turning Chase on, to ascertain her position in his thoughts. Stripping down to a black, lacy push-up bra and changing into the Ducks briefs, she placed a sunflower over her chest. Holding her cellphone high, she reclined, made a pouty face and snapped. Reviewing the photo, she mumbled a curse, certain it wouldn't compete with the glamour centerfolds he drilled daily.

She ransacked her purse, found a flirty fuchsia lipstick and applied it before reattempting. Resting the flower in her cleavage, she placed one seductive finger in her mouth. *Click. Click. Click.* These shots screamed racy perfection. Finding *Darling* in her contacts, she pressed send.

Chapter Ten: Valley Shindigs

Skating through a forest of hardwood trees, Chase followed an end-less frozen river with no one around for miles. It was an overcast, crisp winter day No doubt you could direct if . . . *he heard Morgan's matter-of-fact opinion.*

Passing the same trees, he continued to skate, hearing animals he couldn't place. As he breathed steadily, each exhale frosted in the arctic air. Nothing changed as he gained speed — no vicious beasts attacked, no cracks set him off balance. He wasn't even speeding toward anything.

Finally, Chase swished to stop, sending ice crystals fluttering. He looked down. His hockey skates had unlaced. Casting up, he saw something move down river, too distant to pinpoint. But something was there.

Chase woke sweating heavily, tangled in sheets. Checking the time on his phone, he noticed a text from Morgan Sidney. When he tapped her name, up popped a goddess with bright pink lips, adorned in his gifts. He did a double take.

In New York, Chase had romanticized Morgan, longing to stroke her wavy hair, kiss her freckled nose, scold her for side-eyeing him, press her enticing body against a wall . . . Kali had it right, he was definitely in trouble. So he hadn't reached out.

Once he'd returned to Los Angeles, Kali had invited him to a hockey game. He'd immediately realized it was his and Morgan's rivalry matchup and regretted not planning ahead to take her. Finally acceding to his heart, he'd tried to surprise her with a visit, leaving presents at her doorstep when she wasn't home.

This was a major gesture, since Chase Prince gifted orgasms, not flowers. In the past, his romantic gestures always backfired. His first serious girlfriend, a porn star fifteen years older, had whipped a box of imported chocolates at his face. She was anti-calories. When Chase bought another ex, a dancer, frilly lingerie, she'd insisted the garb must be a recycled costume from set and burned it on the stovetop. Tori had only wanted gifts she chose, fancy objects to be seen and photographed in. He would visit Rodeo Drive to retrieve couture presents she explicitly selected. Fed up, he'd avoided generosities, until Morgan.

Now gaping at her naughty photo, he instinctively considered replying with something dirtier, like links to a scene or two. But he seethed, insulted by her jumbotron kiss. Instead, he jerked off to her photo and went back to sleep.

That week, he sent her calls to voicemail and curved all texts, even a clever *Banana Package* innuendo. Tormented, he barely slept but somehow went a week completely unresponsive to Morgan Sidney's tenacity.

Without a porn feature, Morgan compiled a puff piece. Called *The Name Game*, it studied porn performers' monikers, how they chose them and why. Meanwhile, as she chased Chase, Mandi harassed her, leaving four voicemails that Grant had raved about their date. In her fifth, Mandi suggested a country club double date. At the mere thought, Morgan clutched her work husband's arm and murmured, "I must find the Prince."

"Sweetums," Sean promised, "I'm on it."

That night, resembling Barbie Blue, Morgan toddled up a suburban driveway deep in the Valley dressed in a tight, hot-pink cutout dress and spiky black heels. Sean had found the most *"Gucci"* party in porn and got them dolled up and there within hours. He had even styled her hair voluminously, like a 1970's cover girl.

"Do you think he'll be here?" Morgan asked Sean, who had donned mod non-prescription eyeglasses and a wool fedora.

"Everybody X-rated will be," Sean replied. "Don't worry, we'll find your man."

"He's not *my* man," Morgan insisted.

"Whatever you say."

"I just find it rude to send someone flowers and then ignore them."

As they approached the front stoop of a taupe brick mansion, an enormous bodyguard blocked the doorway. Several characters lined up—two midgets dressed as Santa's elves and a trio in head-to-toe cheetah.

"A little early for Christmas, but late for Halloween," Morgan whispered.

"Sweetums, in smut society, anything goes." As they waited, Sean bounced to electronic music blasting inside.

"Name?" the surly bald bouncer said.

"We're with Trashy Tim," Sean informed him.

"I don't *see* Trashy Tim," the bouncer stated, staring dully.

"Well, no, but—"

"No Tim, no entry," he decreed, fat arms guiding them aside. "Next!"

"Well this is mortifying," Morgan grumbled.

"No soiree rejects Sean Dupriest," Sean declared, entering full-on text mode. "Especially not tawdry Valley shindigs."

"Hey baby!" Tiger Trece shouted, approaching with a young, insanely busty woman on each arm and a couple bros trailing.

"Tiger!" Morgan scuttled over. He kissed both her cheeks but kept his hands on the babes. She whispered, "One of these ladies your wife?"

"Wife?" Tiger asked. "No, no, I'm not married, baby." He

flaunted a vacant ring finger, reassuring his dates, but shot her a sly, shimmering smile. "Why we out here? Let's go in!" Sean scoffed at the bouncer as they followed Tiger's group straight inside. "Find me later, baby," Tiger said, tapping Morgan's tush before disappearing.

They entered to a circus performance in a vast lobby, with quirky, artistic acrobatics. Gothic-like creatures flew between railings and cabaret dancers jived synchronously, avoiding two Harley Davidson bikes beside the main stairwell. As the music shifted from upbeat jazz to a dark, vintage circus beat, the lights reddened for a four-man trampoline act.

Morgan followed Sean to a balcony that overlooked a beat-up pool. Half a dozen giggling girls, with inflated chests squeezed into micro bikinis, played water volleyball. Dudes wearing heavy chain necklaces spectated hungrily. Sean pulled her downstairs, past a hot tub where nude exhibitionists snorted cocaine off each other's chests and navels. Vast glass doors opened to a tiny walkout basement where an amateur DJ spun beats on a dinky mini-stage.

"Tim!" Sean shouted, arms wrapping around a lanky man's purple cashmere scarf.

Scanning the deck, Morgan noted people in a cabana playing some version of strip spin the bottle. When she turned back, Sean and Trashy Tim had vanished. She sighed at Sean's predictability and resolved to hunt down the MIA prince. As she approached the cabana, someone pushed out a chair to stand in her way.

"Ciao, Legs," Kali Sensuale slurred between skinny cigarette drags. Morgan stood a head taller, but Kali sized her up. "Here to pulverize more hearts, civilian?"

"Excuse me?" Morgan shouted over pulsing tracks.

"You heard me. Chase is not here, so you can go crush another soul."

"What are you talking about?" Morgan hailed. "He's

ignoring me. I'm here to find him."

Kali looked skeptical but motioned her to follow. As they walked, Kali's salaciously sliding curves tempted both male and female party guests.

Sitting at a rusted metal table toward the back of the yard, Kali lit another skinny cigarette. "He saw you kissing your man candy at the hockey game," Kali explained, her Italian accent slurred after a few drinks.

Morgan's stomach sank as she took a seat. "It was just one date," she defended. "And I hadn't heard from him all week!"

She leaned forward and glared. "He is more delicate than he seems. Be careful with my best friend."

"Your best friend? Who you also occasionally bang?"

"That is work. I am barely into men." Kali chuckled throatily. "Enough to do scenes, sure, but . . . let me just say, I would rather be with a sexy, skinny girl like you any day."

Morgan shifted uneasily. Kali laughed again to lighten the mood and Morgan joined, chuckling warily and inhaling Kali's cigarette smoke.

"How did you get into this world?" Morgan asked, motioning to the party.

"Nobody ever asks about me," Kali said, softening her posture. "These people only care about themselves."

Morgan nodded her understanding.

"You know, I was always a very sexual girl," Kali admitted. "I came to Los Angeles hoping to make sex my work. So I went online and followed a very, mmm, very shady ad. It said three-thousand dollars for one day of work, modeling for some TV show." Kali dragged on her cigarette.

Morgan kept silent, using her favorite journalism school trick—shut up and they'll keep talking.

Having exhaled the smoke, Kali leaned in to whisper, "So I go to a Hollywood motel. They do not ask for tests, nothing. What did I know, being new? We filmed a threesome and I left. Never got paid. Next day, the phone number was disconnected."

Morgan frowned.

Kali sat upright, lifted her chin and continued, "After this, I vowed to find a good agent. And I did." Her grin gleamed in the darkness. "Now I work with Benny Solomon, who only takes the best girls! We call ourselves *Benny's Babes*, like a club."

"But enough about me, legs," she continued, squeezing Morgan's toned thigh. "Tell me how you are looking like this." So as Kali had revealed her foray into professional pole riding, Morgan detailed her arduous workout regimen.

"Who is that?" Tori Jade squeaked to an industry gal pal, pointing at Kali and Morgan. Dangling tan, scrawny legs over a cracked diving board, Tori scanned social media on her glittery cell phone. When her friends shrugged, Tori pranced to the cabana. "Who's that rando Kali Sensuale is macking on?" she demanded, her full injected lips fixed in a frowny pout.

Looking over, Tiger Trece revealed, "That's Morgan, baby."

"Who? I know everybody in this business."

"She's shadowing Chase for one of those gossip websites."

Tori's purple-contact covered eyes gaped. "A reporter is at this lame mixer?"

Tiger shrugged and returned to his lady friends.

Immediately, Tori tiptoed across the yard, looking like porn royalty in high-heeled white patent boots, a mini leopard-print sarong skirt, and fake breasts swelling out of a black bandeau bra. Chapped makeup, sparkly nails, overstated jewelry and that trademark crystal tiara only added to the effect.

Approaching Morgan and Kali, Tori whined, "If you'd like a real interview, *I'm* your gal." Her spicy perfume emanated.

Kali stood to ask, "The Emperor let you off your leash?"

"Viola doesn't own me, Kali," Tori spouted, then extended a glitter-misted hand to Morgan. "Empress Tori Jade-Emperor, pleased to meet!" Her pitchy voice sounded more pubescent bar mitzvah boy than girlie twenty-nine-year-old XXX star. As Morgan stood and extended a hand, Tori kissed both her cheeks. "Join me for a shot. I'd *so* love to learn about you!"

Morgan looked to Kali.

"Go, go," Kali said, waving them off. "I don't care for this *See You Next Tuesday*. We chat later, legs."

Digging sharp nails into Morgan's arm, Tori guided her to the vacant pool house. She poured two vodka shots at a small bar and carried them to a round, furry sofa bed. They sat, clinked cheers and downed them. "How quaint is this blanket?" Tori squealed, nails digging into the comforter. "I simply must post a photo. Want to be in it?"

"No, thanks," Morgan responded. Since learning Chase had witnessed Grant's swooping smooch, she didn't want to further scathe him. "I'll take one of you." Standing, Morgan grabbed Tori's phone and snapped shots of her reclined legs spread on the bedcover.

Before Morgan could settle back down, Tori snatched it. "Need to keep my *many* followers updated," she bragged, filtering the photo. "Insta, Snap and Twitter are my lifeblood."

Her acrylic nails tapped like her career depended on it. Morgan wiped loose sparkles off her hands and watched fascinated. Eventually, Tori published the picture. Then fixing her hair in the bar mirror, she asked, "Did you hear I'm up for a primetime pilot?" She motioned to the backyard, "I've outgrown this world. No eff-ing way I'll wind up doing granny porn." But her trembling eyes showed more fear than determination.

Morgan nodded along as Tori recounted her journey from trailer trash nobody to industry Princess, now Empress. "I am *so* lucky. I'm doing what hundreds of ratchet loser wannabe girls attempt every year. Except *I* made it!" Then she held out two capsuled MDMA pills. "Want some Molly?"

CHAPTER ELEVEN: ROLEPLAY

Screeching his bike to a halt, Chase Prince parked by the front door. He looked sexily disheveled in faded jeans and a crisp green tee with his leather jacket on top. Everybody stared. Gay, straight, bi, trans or still deciding, nearly everyone wanted to ride him.

A man on a mission, he paced through the house, ignoring anybody who attempted to chat him up. People were always approaching him with questionable *investment opportunities*. Everybody wanted something from the kid with the face, or in his case, the shaft. He'd learned that lesson early on.

Chase spotted Kali smoking out back. "Where are they?" he demanded.

"Bambino, is nice to see you, too."

"Kali," he growled. He'd been cozily in bed just half an hour earlier when Kali texted a photo of his ex cuddling up to Morgan. Kali nodded to a sloppy crowd dancing and humping in the basement. Chase hurried over to where Tori and Morgan grinded obscenely, cheek to cheek.

Transported to a euphoric, blissful state, Morgan luxuriated in the flashing lights, savoring Tori's soft skin and perceiving every bass drop. Her legs were putty, like a jellyfish.

His jaw clenched as he marched over to rip them apart. "What the fuck is going on?" he shouted.

"Darling!" Morgan proclaimed.

"Let's get out of here," he insisted.

"Who are you, her dad?" Tori retorted, kissing Morgan's cheek.

"Just . . . *hers* . . ." he trailed off.

Morgan resembled a dolphin, smiling wide as she leaned to kiss him. She noted zero hints of whiskey or beer permeating his sweet, minty breath.

"Let's talk," he said, clutching Morgan's hand and pointing at Tori. "Stay away."

Tori observed curiously, jealously, as Chase cupped Morgan's nape and led her outside. Alongside the house they passed some stoners getting high, all of whom checked Morgan out obviously. She didn't notice, but Chase eyed them.

As he led her to the driveway, she fondled his chest. "This is the softest eff-ing shirt I've ever touched." Another wave of ecstasy overcame her and she continued rubbing grandiosely with both hands. Her eyes circled back. These were the *rolling* Molly highs she'd heard about. Grinning like a clam, she swayed in the cool air.

"What are you on, Morg?"

"MDMA!" she exclaimed, still caressing him.

"Tori made you do this?"

She rolled her eyes. "No, dingus. Molly and I go way back!"

"Dingus?" He laughed. "So you've done Molly before?"

"No," she confessed. "But I've wanted to. Tori just gave it to me."

"Of course." His nostrils blazed. "To loosen you up, so you'll adore her and proclaim her wonderfulness. Everything that bitch does is calculated." He approached his bike. "Why would you even talk to her? I don't want people from my seedy realm corrupting you."

"I'm here for work."

"Says the girl on Molly."

She sighed. "How could I pass an opportunity to meet your supposedly snakelike evil queen ex?"

He shrugged and snapped on his helmet.

"Do we have to leave?" she asked.

"I'm out. *Someone* suggested I party less." Chase offered a spare helmet. "You're welcome to join me."

Flattered he'd taken her advice, her heart tingled. And despite sober Morgan's belief that motorcycles were dangerous, she grabbed the helmet. In that moment, she needed speed and life on the edge. Her skimpy dress rode up as she wobbled onto the bike. Yanking it down, she attempted to conceal her butt cheeks.

"You all right?" Chase asked, handing over his leather jacket.

She put it on, hugged his stomach and inhaled. "You smell like body wash."

He chuckled as they vroomed down the driveway.

Twenty-five minutes later he parked outside his apartment.

"I need you, naked, now," Morgan asserted, climbing off as a sharp wave of euphoria moved her. She craved nothing more than his hands commanding her body.

But he edged away when she tried to kiss him. "Let's go inside," he said. Cleo hopped up as they entered and Morgan plopped down to tickle her, cherishing the soft fur.

His apartment no longer resembled Thirsty Thursdays at a frat house — no wild pre-game or after-party remnants, just a soda glass on a coaster. Carpets had been vacuumed and counters wiped. He'd even hung window curtains.

Chase sat on the sofa. "Can we talk?"

Her eyes undressed him. "Can we bang?"

With a smirk, he palmed his forehead.

"You look delicious," she stated. "And I am starving." Licking her lips, she strutted forward slowly and cooed, "I know . . . that you want to know . . . what turns me on." Biting her lip, she leaned toward him, cleavage on display. "I want to play pretend, Chase." She placed a finger in her mouth and sucked seductively.

But he stepped away. "I'm not doing this while you're rolling."

She hung her head. On Molly, his rejection stung harder, turning her pure bliss into anxious inadequacy.

When she looked up, he scowled and said, "Plus dating another guy, apparently."

"I am not," she asserted. "Kali mentioned you saw the kiss cam. It was one meaningless date. Besides, you *bang* other women daily."

"That's my job, Morgan. If you want to be together, you have to be comfortable with that."

"Be together?" Leaning on a barstool, she shut her eyes.

"Let's go to sleep," Chase said, taking her hand. He led her to the bedroom and handed her a jersey cotton t-shirt.

She changed in the bathroom. Finding cleanser wipes, she removed clumpy makeup. The gloppy smiley face on the towelette resembled a clown. In the mirror, her natural face, simple and pretty, stared back at her.

As the MDMA wore off, her heightened emotions waned from upbeat to emptiness, like a chorus fading out. She burrowed into bed beside Chase. He draped an arm around her shoulders as she curled up tight and rubbed the fair hairs on his forearm.

Dreaming of eggs and coffee, Chase opened his eyes and inhaled scents of both. Entering the kitchen wearing only briefs, he watched Morgan bounce in his oversized blue t-shirt and a thong, whistling to a house music song. She spun around and, spotting him, gasped and tilted the pan, sending scrambled eggs flying.

"Not a problem," he said. "I'll just have you for breakfast." Lunging forward, he pecked her cheek.

But she edged him away. "Last night you wanted to talk. Now, it's my turn."

Obligingly, he sat on a barstool but eyed her hungrily.

"If you'd like me to open up and divulge my desires, then you have to open up, too. Don't shut me out and ignore me for days. Tell me if you want to be exclusive."

"I do want you to myself," he admitted.

Spinning her bangle bracelets, she responded, "Me too."

"Well sex is my job." he added. "You have to be comfortable with that."

Morgan picked up a rag and started cleaning the messy floor. After tossing egg clusters in the trash, she scrubbed the counter. Both lips curled as she focused intently.

His hand stopped hers. "What are you thinking?"

Casting her gaze up, she explained, "That speedbumps and potholes obstruct the road ahead."

He tilted his head. "But does the journey still thrill you?"

She tossed the rag in the sink and sat on the stool next to his. "A month ago, I'd have considered penetrating other women cheating, no question."

"And now?"

"I'd like to try to get comfortable with it. After visiting set, I see how unromantic shooting porn is. It's work for you, I understand that. But will you be sleeping with your exes? Because that is not okay."

"Never," he assured. "Performers are never booked together after breakups. Benny knows. Every director in town knows I won't touch Tori again. Ever."

Morgan nodded.

"That everything?" he asked, nuzzling her neck.

"For now."

He sucked her earlobe, then dragged his teeth down her neck, lips brushing her collarbone. "Good, because I have a second fantasy to fulfill."

"Ever tried one of these?" Morgan asked with a smirk, lifting an artificial vagina.

"Darling, I've tried it all," he said, winking. "But we're here for you." He picked a bullet vibrator off a display and held it out.

She shrugged as they continued along a leash and cock ring wall at Chase's favorite adult toy store. She'd never before set foot in a sex shop. Her ex had brought toys into the bedroom, but they'd never shopped together.

Morgan grabbed a Chase Prince imitation scepter toy and asked, "When's my turn with the real wand of wonder?"

Silently, he returned it to the mantel. Instead he seized a branded Prince of Sin penis vibrator, made to mold. "Why don't you test ride this? Let me know if my product is true to form."

"Why use a piece of rubber when you own the bull?" She checked out his real package and grinned, eyes crinkling coyly.

As they approached costumes, Chase lifted a skimpy maid getup. "Care to fluff my pillow?"

Morgan shook her head.

"I think you may need an injection," he said, choosing a male doctor outfit.

She breathed a small chuckle but wrinkled her nose.

"Morg, this only works if you disclose *what* you want to roleplay."

She scanned an overwhelmingly cluttered wall of innocent schoolgirls, naughty nurses . . . seemingly boundless options.

"Can I change my fantasy?" Fidgeting with her bracelet, she considered feigning saucy enthusiasm for handcuffs or whipped cream.

"Didn't we just discuss being open and honest this morning?"

"I don't care to do this anymore," she grumbled, storming outside. She perched on a wooden bench, elbows on her thighs.

Wind chimes jangled as Chase left the store. His eyes locked with a mother pushing a baby carriage. Recognizing him, she blushed and scurried away.

"I thought we were just having fun, darling," Chase said, sitting beside Morgan.

She kicked stones toward the street. "It's embarrassing."

"It doesn't have to be."

As his hand tenderly squeezed hers, she took a deep breath. "I've never told anyone my fantasies. With my ex it was always whatever he needed."

"It's your turn to get what you want. If you'll tell me."

"It's awkward. And I'm scared you'll associate it with someone I hate and definitely don't fantasize about. Or you'll think it's bad or I'm sick or—"

"Morgan," he cut her off, moving his hand to her thigh. "Your fantasies shouldn't provoke guilt."

"I don't feel guilty, just . . . inhibited."

"Well if you aren't ready, we don't need to do this."

She wanted to be ready, to bolster herself up and force doubt from memory. Refusing to back down, she grasped his arm and confessed, "I've always had a boss-secretary fantasy."

Chase widened that movie-star grin. "That's what you were afraid to tell me? Morg, it's a pretty common one."

"I didn't want you thinking it had to do with Jason, my real boss," she confessed. "Because I cannot stand him."

"Fantasies aren't real-life. That's why they're fantasies. Exploring them with partners you trust makes it fun. Creating a safe space, away from reality."

With that, she unwound, accepting that her own needs weren't just valid, but vital, and continued. "When I was twelve or thirteen, I found a DVD of the film *Secretary*. It belonged to our housekeeper, Rosa. Watching it, I grew so turned on. That was the first time I masturbated." Morgan bit her lip. She'd never told anybody that story.

"Well then, let's find you a pencil skirt, Ms. Secretary," Chase responded, winking cheekily.

Instead of a sex toy parlor, they went shopping at a chic department store. Afterward Chase turned his motorcycle to return to his place, but Morgan suggested someplace more fitting.

"Miss Sidney. My office. Now!" Chase bellowed from the *Slander* conference room, where just weeks earlier Morgan had first considered nibbling his lower lip. How she'd resisted, she'd never know. One thing she did know was that Jason had everyone work from home on weekends.

Morgan breathed deeply and entered the conference room leaving little to the imagination in an obscenely low-cut purple blouse and tight black pencil skirt that hugged her thighs. Her perched messy bun sat as rumpled as the paperwork she carried. After placing the documents before him, she slammed the hefty door shut.

Chase sat reading a magazine, feet propped on the glass tabletop with colorful banana-patterned socks peeking out from leather loafers. He looked younger than thirty in round, full-rim eyeglasses. But he embodied power and style, wearing slim fit dress pants, a silk button up and sleek skinny tie.

"Finally," he huffed, completely in character, leering as he folded the magazine. "How difficult is it to make a few photocopies?" His almost-emerald eyes glowered, and she laughed awkwardly. But he returned a growl. "This isn't a joke!"

"S-sorry Chase," she stammered, staring at her glossy, pointed-toe heels while nervously shifting side to side. Blood surged to her head, cheeks reddening.

"That's Mr. Prince," he corrected, all domineering boss.

Her insides quivered, startled and aroused, exactly how she'd imagined.

"God, can't you do anything right?" Standing to scowl down, he ultimately glanced lower, savoring her brimming V-neck. Pausing for a moment, he admired her shapely chest, the round, natural breasts he'd first noticed on their hike. Then he shook the papers. "These aren't even double-sided, *whore.*"

Suddenly, Morgan dropped character and spun to face the door. "One second," she said, leaning against the door to inhale a deep breath.

"What's wrong?" He clutched her shoulder. When she didn't respond, he decided, "We're stopping."

"No, no, no. You just can't use that word."

"What word? Whore?"

A jolt. "Yes."

"Okay. Care to elaborate?"

Facing him, she shivered, eyes pleading not to probe. "Let's just continue."

He kissed her forehead. "Darling, we definitely need a safe word moving forward."

"I already feel safe."

"You know what I mean."

"Fine, let's use *dingus,*" she suggested.

Chase chuckled. "You have to use it, if you need to."

"So do you," she challenged.

He smirked, trusting her. "Now, Miss Sidney," he proceeded, hissing and lifting a sheet of paper.

"It's actually *Ms.,*" she retorted.

"All right, *Ms.* Sidney. Why aren't these double-sided?"

"It must have been the copier!" she defended, snapping into character.

He tossed the stack, sheets rustling and scattering onto the table, chairs and floor. "God forbid you could check your work before handing it over to your boss!"

She looked to her feet.

"Let me show you how a photocopier works." Clasping her forearm, he led her to the copy machine. "But what can we copy? Hmmm." He switched the machine on and it zinged to life. "I know." Standing behind Morgan, he reached around and unbuttoned her blouse.

"Mr. Prince!" she shrilled, feeling lascivious but turning to slap his hand, because that was what a real secretary would do.

"Are you no longer interested in that promotion?" His brows raised.

Morgan side-eyed at their scene's familiarity.

"Did you just side-eye me? I'm your *boss*." Whipping Morgan around again, he finished loosening her blouse to reveal a feminine black balconette bra. He slid her shirt down and dropped it to the floor. "Let's show you how to use a photocopier." Chase fisted Morgan's bun and pressed her chest against the cool glass panel. The machine beeped as he added ten copies and hit Start. It flashed, hummed and droned, spitting out colored prints of *Ms.* Sidney's bursting chest.

When it finally stopped, he released her and she twisted back to face him. "Are you done, Mr. Prince?" Her dark brown eyes glowered into his. She squinted, realizing his irises were two different shades — one green, one hazel.

"I'm just getting started."

Morgan leaned desperately into his mouth, kissing fervently and gnawing on that lower lip. But he pulled away, slammed the copier cover down and lifted her right onto it. His steady hands slid under her skirt, up smooth thighs. "Should I distribute these documents at our next team meeting?" he asked.

"You're perverted."

Reaching her thong, he ran two fingers over the dampening fabric. "Your body seems to like that about me. Beg me not to pass them around the office."

"You wouldn't," she dared.

He grunted in response, carefully inching the skirt down her legs, then lifting her off the machine. She shrieked playfully until he placed her on the conference table. As she reclined on her elbows, he angled forward. Their mouths grazed, then he nibbled from flush lips to her neck and collarbone.

With closed eyes, she welcomed his steady fingers slipping each bra strap over her shoulders. As his soft lips pecked her chest, he reached behind to unclasp her bra. She shivered as it fell to the floor, cool air chilling her nipples.

At last she peeled her eyelids open to an authoritative, aroused gaze. His hazel eye matched his ashen shirt while the green eye resembled a vivid forest. Morgan wondered how she'd overlooked their charm and longed to learn all his other subtleties.

Their hands entwined, Chase tugged her upright. "Now that I have you stirred up, Ms. Sidney, it's your turn." He guided her hands under his waistband to an expanding erection, then unfastened his shirt with an arrogant swagger.

"You're my boss!" she whined. "I'll go to Human Resources."

He lifted a cleavage printout and said, "And I'll tell HR you're stalking me, sending me dirty photos like the dirty little girl you are."

"That is not fair!"

"Life's not fair, Ms. Sidney."

In real life she'd storm out on such a repulsive boss, but this felt fun, safe and hot. She stood and whirled him against the table. Then she kneeled, unbuttoned his slacks and unleashed the engorged beast.

Pressing forward, she sucked the tip. He gripped her hair and thrust further down her throat. With a gag, she pulled away.

"Dingus?" Chase asked concernedly, realizing how aggressive he'd gotten. She looked up with bold brown eyes that teetered between tough and delicate.

"No, Mr. Prince," Ms. Sidney responded. "But hands to yourself. I'd like to earn my promotion." Morgan removed a small tub of coconut oil from her purse and twisted the lid. "A friend of mine does porn. He says this stuff's all the rage." As she scooped oil onto her fingers, she winked at him, then rubbed it on his cock.

"You fraternize with porn stars?" he asked. "I knew you were filthy."

She grinned in response, twisting oily hands around his heavy shaft. He'd used oil as lubricant during sex but never on its own. Eyes closed, Chase enjoyed the warm, buttery massage of the surprisingly underrated lubed hand job.

Suddenly, an urge to burst pulsated through his veins. It surprised him, since jizzing on set had become, well, hard recently. Getting with other women, even for work, had felt like cheating on Morgan.

If Chase came now, he'd struggle on set later. So to avoid technical difficulties in studio, he pulled her up. He didn't want Morgan to feel guilty for affecting his game, so he didn't explain.

"Your turn," he stated, sitting her on the table and peeling her thong down.

Kneeling, he kissed downward from her belly button and slipped two fingers into her slick opening. His tongue pressed up, down and around an engorged clit.

Her body twitched. No man had ever navigated it so precisely. He took a condom from his pant pocket, rolled it on and glided inside her. She moaned as he stretched and filled her wholly, then she placed his finger in her mouth and nibbled.

As their grinding hastened, his free hand thumbed her clit. "Do you like that, Ms. Sidney?"

Face tight, her legs clenched.

"Ms. Sidney?"

Purring, she hunched her back to drive his shaft deeper.

He seesawed through her abundant wetness, rocking back and forth, then instructed, "Cum for your boss."

She wailed, orgasm rippling, muscles clamping around his cock. As she collapsed to catch her breath, he pulled out.

His sneer widened. "From the day I hired you, Ms. Sidney, I knew I'd get you on your back." He removed the condom, wrapped it in paper, then pulled up his briefs and jeans.

"You didn't finish," Morgan half stated, half asked.

"I'm taping in a few hours. Need to save my load."

Her stomach churned with a reminder that he'd soon be roleplaying with another woman, or five. "I thought you were a pro?" she asked.

"Sorry." Chase's hand met her shoulder. "It's the trade I chose."

"Gotcha." She winced, but found her clothing. Once dressed, she collected the scattered papers, sashayed from the conference room and slipped them into the office paper shredder. It vroomed shaving them to bits.

"There's some time before I need to head to the studio," he said.

Hands intertwined, they approached the elevator and she pressed up. The door dinged and they stepped inside. Across the room, peering over a shaded corner cubicle, sat Morgan's rival, Marcus Rodd, leering as the doors clicked shut.

High above Century City, under a bright afternoon sky,

Morgan and Chase snuggled on the rooftop deck. Splayed on a large outdoor sofa, they nestled together like Cinderella's glass slipper, finally securing that one, perfect fit.

Morgan considered his commitment to their scene, how he'd encouraged her to admit her fantasy and ascertained her comfort throughout. She wanted to boast his amazingness, including what she compared him against, but going there would wreck the calm.

"This is the type of porn I'd love to direct," he confided.

"Spooning on balconies?" Facing him, she giggled.

"Real couples having real sex," he explained. "First times with somebody new. Makeup sex. You, rolling a condom on with your mouth or blushing admitting fantasies. Not that flashy, plastic, facial crap I star in."

He pecked her still-swollen lips. "I dream of capturing moments like this, when the person you're with has never looked more exquisite. Real attraction and beautiful, primal desire."

"Do it!" she encouraged, straddling his lap and nuzzling an unsure, locked jaw. "You really should. Talk to Jimmy, or whoever's in charge of that. You'd be amazing." As he sighed, she examined his hesitant eyes. "You know, one of your eyes is hazel."

Chase's heart swelled. Not one ex ever had noticed his eye colors. He realized Morgan saw things others never had and wondered if maybe she did know his capabilities. "You know," he said, kissing her again, "you have a freckle on your upper lip."

He inhaled her signature vanilla swirled with post-sex sweat. Chase had never felt tranquil with a woman. But since Morgan didn't have one-eighty mood swings or demand fancy gifts or whip furniture, for once he could just be.

They made out playfully. It was one of those too-rare, peaceful moments in their hectic lives. Despite concerns about family approval or job complexities, it seemed like things might work out. Like nothing stood their way.

"I must be booked with Chase Prince!" Tori Jade barked into her sparkly cellphone. No longer squeaky, bubbly Tori, this ass-naked businesswoman schemed behind a residential house on steep foothills deep in the Valley.

Nearby, seven giggly nude girls wearing strap-on dildos splashed on an inflatable waterslide next to a colorful bouncy castle. A cameraman directed, "Give her cock a suck" and "Stick your face in her tush." Tori Jade topped the bill in this lesbian orgy, which from the street looked like a two-year-old's birthday party.

"We thought you were only shooting girl-girl now," her agent's assistant remarked.

"I'm making chump change," Tori spewed. "There's no money in muff diving."

"Ummm . . ." The assistant faltered. "Will Chase's camp agree to this?"

"Lie if you must," Tori demanded. "I don't give a rat's ass how. Fuck Viola. Forcing me to book minor league girl-on-girl-on-ten-more-girls gigs." She huffed, clicking off. Suffocating on snatch, Tori craved a stiff hog.

Chapter Twelve: That's Where You'll Stay

Chase shuffled into the Lit Empire Entertainment head-quarters. Back when it was Clay's Empire, his first shoot had taped there. It had been alongside Ella Vogue, who later became his much-older girlfriend. Anxiously, he'd slinked through the polished lobby and got lost, confusing dozens of private sets and stages. Once he'd finally located Dungeon #3, some jaded director had patronized him for being new and destined to fail. It pushed Chase to disprove the guy's theory that new performers always blew their loads too soon. Chase had held his, cumming on command inside Ella, as cream pies were trendy then. A hard-earned reputation thrived from there.

Nowadays, the palatial Lit Empire complex was Chase's second home. He'd boned in nearly every room, not just on sets but in offices, storage closets and even on the roof. But ever since Morgan had encouraged his director dreams, he'd obsessively considered a sabbatical. Finally, he'd arranged a meeting with CEO Viola Emperor.

Heart racing, he headed for Viola's office holding an over-stuffed three-ring binder. Though he'd taped scenes at Lit Empire since the breakup, he and Viola hadn't crossed paths since everything went down.

He opened the door to Viola's newest secretary, a busty, young strawberry blonde chafed by a leather dog collar. Viola was notorious for running through hot little secretaries faster than milk cartons.

Cheeks pink, the girl led Chase through a tiny foyer to Viola's laughably overdone office. A regal purple rug cloaked wooden floors, her purple throne desk chair bore golden posts, and thick velour curtains framed a window overlooking a parking structure.

Staring outside, Viola belted, "Welcome, welcome," before turning around grandiosely. Tall, pale and big boned, forty-something Viola wore her short hair dyed bright red. "Please, sit." She gestured to a peasant chair across from her dark oak desk. He adjusted in the squeaky, stiff seat while Viola fell leisurely into an elevated, cushioned throne.

"I am truly pleased you called this meeting," Viola continued, "I'm so glad the whole, er, incident, hasn't wrenched our relationship."

They both knew Lit Empire was screwed without its most popular performer. Chase had been tight with Viola's father, Clay, who'd spent decades building his empire. A risk taker, Clay had purchased countless website domains, then packaged subscriptions. He'd embraced change, helping the company flourish with internet streaming, where many others failed.

Clay had died suddenly of a heart attack five years earlier. Viola hadn't touched business development since, leaving Lit Empire's model hugely outdated. Other companies stayed relevant releasing apps and virtual reality porn, while Lit Empire Entertainment didn't even have one central website.

"That incident where you eloped with my girlfriend?" Chase asked.

"Er, yes." She coughed uncomfortably. "So, what brought you to see the Emperor?"

"Business."

"Okay," Viola responded suspiciously. She never discussed business with performers, only agents.

After a deep breath, Chase stated, "I'd like to direct."

"Why?" Viola blurted.

"I need a challenge. And I have so many ideas." Placing his binder on the desk, he opened it.

"Do you?" Her hands curled into shaky fists.

Chase stood enthusiastically. "A lot of what we create is, well, tacky. And degrading. Imagine porn for everyone. For women and couples and—"

"Our content sells just fine."

"Does it?" he asked. Everybody knew Lit Empire was deep in the red.

"Lit Empire viewers don't care for gentlemen treating women nicely," she explained. "They want bitches and hos taking face shots and begging for more."

"I think you're wrong," Chase said, opening the binder. "I've been researching the market."

He detailed statistics about potential target markets, both men and women who struggled but wanted to find porn that wasn't misogynistic—and were willing to pay for it. He'd analyzed relatively limited competitors and explained how the same budget Lit Empire put into a regular scene could produce higher quality product.

"We could start small, with one or two scenes, to see how it does. And advertise to couples, get them watching together."

"Enough!" Viola slammed her hands down, stood and paced to the door. "We're no PG-thirteen, softcore company."

"It doesn't have to be PG-thirteen. Or even softcore. We could—"

"Cut the *we* crap. You are a performer, an outstanding performer, really, truly. But that's where you'll stay." She opened the door and shooed him out.

He took his binder and left.

Relaxing on a campy wooden lawn chair in the serene Venice garden café, Morgan remained clueless about her feature. She'd temporarily held Jason off with her porn name puff piece. Tiger Trece and Kali Sensuale had contributed video clips explaining the meanings behind their aliases. Other performers had followed suit until Morgan's three-minute video featured a dozen porn stars. They'd all retweeted the link and it reached a quarter million views in twenty-four hours. Satisfied with the hits, Jason had extended her feature another week.

She opened her laptop and logged onto a free XXX site she'd been frequenting for research. Only for research, as she hadn't viewed porn for pleasure since her ex. Scanning through her notes, she noticed a star beside Tiger Trece's name.

Morgan Googled *African Americans in Porn* and *Porn Race Inequality*. She read a few articles and message boards. When she pressed *More* below a tab, a giant vagina and the words *GET MORE PUSSY* bombarded the screen. A woman's moans blasted from her laptop speakers as the dozen or so café patrons stared.

Tap, tap, tapping the ESC key, Morgan flushed. The volume escalated. Sweat seeped through her skin. Finally, she slammed the computer shut. It took an extra beat, but finally the wailing ceased.

Silence followed, the calm terrace vibe scandalized. Morgan mouthed, *Sorry* to onlookers and shrugged defeatedly. An older woman offered a compassionate nod as Morgan packed her knapsack and scurried away.

Shortly thereafter, Morgan cuddled under a white Peruvian alpaca throw at home while web chatting with Jadine at antivirus support in Singapore. Listening to an edgy electropop album, she watched Jadine run remote laptop scans and delete malware files.

"How do you use this computer?" Jadine asked.

"For work, mostly," Morgan explained vaguely, as the GET MORE PUSSY file popped up. "I'm doing a work assignment on pornography."

"Mmm-hmm," Jadine responded. She'd heard that excuse before.

Morgan watched as Jadine discovered seemingly endless malware files, like HORNY VAG and FUCKING 'N FISTING. Two hours later, as the sun set and Jadine finished up, someone knocked at the front door.

Through the peephole, Morgan spotted Chase. His sudsy scent billowed in as he entered wearing dark jeans and his leather jacket over a crisp black t-shirt. Despite his formal attire, with three days' worth of stubble the man still belonged on a rock album cover. Morgan admired her smoldering boyfriend.

His lips met hers, then he returned an ogle. She donned casual harem pants and fluffy rainbow slippers, with hair sticking up in several directions. "This what you're wearing to dinner?" he asked. "Not that I mind, darling."

"Sorry, I forgot our plans," she said, checking the laptop. "I'm online with Jadine."

Chase lifted a brow. "Jadine?"

"My new cyber pen pal. We're sexting."

"Really?" His face lit up.

"We might as well be. She already found my horny vag."

"What?"

Morgan erupted laughing as the technician finished scanning. "My computer got a virus," she explained. "But that was only the tip of the iceberg. Apparently, it had malware built up, likely from researching you, darling."

"Lucky for you, that's the only virus I'm circulating," he rebutted with a wink. "Got my test results today. I received clearance for two more weeks."

"Please don't wink all charming while confirming you're STD-free."

"I'm Prince Chase, not Prince Charming."

"Ha. Cute," she replied sardonically, typing a thank you to Jadine before closing the malware-free laptop and joining him on the sofa. "We're still using condoms."

Morgan had been taking the birth control pill for many years and in past committed relationships, had ditched condoms once she and her partner got tested. But dating someone who boinked for a living, a test every other week wasn't reliable enough for her to abandon rubbers.

"Whatever you desire, darling," he responded as she snuggled under his arm.

"Jadine also set up anti-theft protection. Want to be my emergency contact?"

"A true honor," he replied, rendering his phone.

She installed the app, then grabbed his unshaven face and sucked that delectable lower lip. He hummed and cupped her soft breasts over a loose tank top. She sighed as he leaned away and said, "As much as I'd love to strip you down, we have to go."

But she kissed him forcefully, tugging his wavy hair. He pecked her nose before groaning and standing. "Fine," she lamented, moving to her bedroom but leaving the door open so they could still chat.

He explored her pad, unsurprised by its tidiness. "Did you collect all these artifacts yourself?" he asked, admiring a handwoven dreamcatcher.

"Mostly," she shouted, slipping into a dress. "And my Dad always brought me knickknacks from his work trips. I started collecting my own as I travelled more."

Growing up, Chase's mom didn't have extra cash for trips. Now he could afford to travel, but rarely got away, often working Thanksgiving, Christmas and Fourth of July. And his exes never cared to leave California, unless it was for gigs or events. Occasionally Chase travelled for work, to New York, Paris, Australia . . . but hardly took time to explore. Twelve fast years in porn had flashed by. Chase wondered if Morgan could slow the journey. He imagined them travelling the world together, visiting tropical paradises and accumulating knickknacks while fulfilling her fantasies on every continent.

Morgan switched off the music and emerged in a silky knee-length gray dress that hugged her curves. Sporting a high stylish loose bun and minimal makeup with glossed lips, she struck a showy pose.

He catcalled his approval. Just then, a miniature Big Ben clock chimed on the bureau. 8:00. "Shoot. We're late. I told her eight." His hand met the small of Morgan's neck as he guided her outside.

"Told who?"

Chapter Thirteen: Ms. Sandra Krol

Chase turned his motorcycle onto a quiet residential street on the Mar Vista Hill. Two miles inland from Venice Beach, the westside Mar Vista neighborhood boasted tree-lined properties, Farmer's Markets, soaring property values and, for lucky homeowners on the hill, sunsets overlooking the sparkling Pacific.

With Morgan's arms hugging his waist, Chase pulled into the driveway of a Mid-Century Modern Eichler-style ranch with vertical siding and a flat roof. After parking, he led her through a fenced-in yard secluded by trees, with colorful vintage courtyard furniture decorating a vast stone patio. Chase casually pulled a glass sliding door open to enter the house.

With an open, airy floor plan, lauan paneling and glass skylights, the interiors were as architecturally deliberate as the exterior. Despite the home's of-an-era style, Morgan first noticed a framed drawing of a woman touching herself displayed on the wall.

"Baby!" the slender Sandra Krol gushed, emerging around a corner, arms opened. Her round, clear blue eyes widened behind octagon spectacles as she grasped Chase's face to kiss both cheeks. Barefoot and barefaced, she wore a floral maxi dress, beaded jewelry and flowing white hair with slight blonde streaks, tokens of her youth. Once a flower child, this sixty-something hippie was Chase Prince's mom. "Who is this?"

"Ma, this is Morgan, who I've been telling you about."

"Right, of course, Harrison."

Harrison. His birth name. Morgan only knew him as Chase. She also hadn't known they'd be meeting his mother tonight. It both miffed and flattered her. "Hi Mrs . . ." Morgan trailed. She didn't know her boyfriend's actual surname.

"*Ms.* Sandra Krol." Sandra half-smiled before returning to her son. "Come, sit. I put out soda."

Morgan followed them to a retro daybed sofa, searching mother and son for resemblances. On a bookshelf nearby, she noticed a clay sculpture of two women and a man in nude embrace. All the artwork directly contrasted the modest, traditional pieces at her parents' house. She'd craved this sort of liberated atmosphere growing up, a space where sex wasn't suppressed.

Several framed photos of Chase rested beside the statue. One was of a younger Chase and Sandra clad in matching, paint-covered overalls, painting murals on a building. Another showed toddler Chase watching a movie with a popcorn bucket half his size on his lap. Morgan wished she could have known her man as a boy.

"So, Morgan," Sandra began, handing over an organic root beer, "what do you do for a living?"

"I write. I'm a journalist. And yourself?"

"A journalist? For which publication?" Sandra patted a stack of magazines and newspapers. "We are avid readers."

As Morgan looked for signs of a companion, Sandra squeezed her son into a side hug. By *we*, she'd meant herself and Chase, or rather, Harrison. "Well, I'm more of a digital vlogger," Morgan explained. "Hoping to produce soon."

"She works for *Slander*," he added.

Sandra sneered. "Oh right, the gossip *vlogger*."

"Ma," Chase urged.

"No, no." Morgan explained, "It's not just gossip, it's . . ."

"Gossip vlogs are merely your generation's Page Six." Sandra sipped her drink.

"She posted that profile on me," he bragged.

"The one highlighting your depression?" Sandra asked.

Morgan gulped.

"At least it was honest," he defended. "And her last video just reached one million views in less than a week!"

"One million?" Sandra's eyes narrowed. "That makes you a *journalist* who is sleeping with her subject?"

Morgan tugged a bangle bracelet. Her honey vanilla deodorant wasn't strong enough for the sweat this woman provoked. "Well, Chase, or Harrison, and I started dating *after* that profile. Now I'm researching the industry as a whole."

"I'm showing Morg the ropes. Helping her navigate my domain."

Sandra clutched Chase into another tight embrace. "Well that is nice of you, baby." But she turned back to Morgan. "Where were you raised?"

"Orange County, near Lake Forest. And yourself?"

"Has my son met your family?"

"Um, not yet . . ." Morgan's family had no idea Chase existed.

Sandra tsked quietly and clasped Chase's knee. "How is work, baby?"

"Same old," he responded, scratching behind his neck. He hadn't told either of them about Viola Emperor's disheartening decree that he'd never be more than a schlong.

"Maybe it's time you retired?" Sandra scratched his back.

Chase quickly stood and asked, "Do you still need me to look at that sink?"

Sandra sighed before he disappeared down a hallway.

"You're encouraging him to retire?" Morgan asked.

"*I* was an active member of the feminist art movement," she boasted. Sandra had encouraged his retirement since he shot his first . . . shot. "Do you think I appreciate my son appointing women hos, then *splooging* on their faces?"

Morgan followed Sandra as she carried the drink tray into a mod kitchen with matte black cabinets, a dark stone island and mixed-metal knobs and handles. She sat on a cushioned banquette.

"Your home is lovely," Morgan hailed.

Sandra checked the vegan casserole in the oven, ignoring Morgan with a glacial temperament frostier than the cubes in their drinks.

"I can't imagine baby, um, Harrison running through this place in diapers."

"Probably because he did not."

"No?"

"My son purchased my home a decade ago." She handed over a photo of herself, younger and chipper, holding an infant in front of a scratched apartment door. "On Harrison's first birthday, we moved into that lousy walk-up, in a neighborhood much less secure than this. As I taught art and took awful odd jobs to make rent, my son insisted he would use his means to better our lives. Harrison cares for me and I will always look out for him." Sandra stared Morgan down before shouting through the open doorway. "Baby, how is that drain coming?"

Morgan strayed to the living room and fixated on a watercolor painting of Chase and Sandra. "See any resemblance?" Chase asked, rubbing her shoulders from behind. She shook no. "Apparently I'm a clone of my dad."

"Where's he?" Morgan faced him.

"Ma insists she doesn't remember so much as a name, just the vagueness of a face identical to mine. One green eye. One hazel."

"And you believe that?"

He shrugged. "Her story's never changed."

"Does that bother you?" Morgan frowned.

Again, his shoulders lifted. "At least I had one caring

parent, who I'm aware is behaving standoffish."

"She's no fairy godmother," Morgan responded. "Also, you could have prefaced dinner with, 'by the way, want to meet my mother tonight?"

His eyes wandered. "I was nervous you'd think things were moving too fast. Sorry. I'm a jerk." He kissed her forehead. "Pardon me, please? I beg. I plead."

Morgan side-eyed him, but smirked her clemency.

During dinner, Sandra loosened up slightly, though mostly ignoring Morgan to reminisce with Chase. He perceived the hostile vibes and suggested they skip dessert since he had an early shoot.

"Bye, baby," Sandra said, opening the front door. She kissed his cheek and they hugged tight.

"Thanks for having me, Ms. Krol," Morgan said, avoiding eye contact and rushing to Chase's motorcycle.

"What's with you tonight?" Chase asked.

"With me?" Sandra gazed off in a mix of defensiveness and embarrassment. "Nothing is *with me*."

"Ma. You've always been amicable with my exes."

"This one is bright. Too bright." Sandra sighed, facing him. "The others were harmless dimwits, besides leeching onto your wealth and notoriety."

"You know I'll always take care of my finances, and yours."

Sandra lifted a hand to shush him. "I am not concerned about money. One million views in one week? *This one* has the power and means to hurt you on a vast scale. I am merely concerned."

"*Morgan* is bright. Something I value. I've met my match."

"I appreciate that she challenges you, but you'll always be my baby." She pinched his cheek.

"Okay," Chase exhaled. "Hopefully with time, you'll see her as I do. Night, Ma." He hugged her again before meeting

Morgan out front.

As they drove away, Morgan peered over her shoulder and spotted Sandra winking before she sealed the door. It was the same coy wink that Chase carried like none other.

CHAPTER FOURTEEN: RELINQUISHING CONTROL

As per Morgan's text, Chase entered a plain office building in the industrial Santa Monica quarter. Past dusk on a weeknight, it was deserted, work done for the day. He found a unit with no name or title posted and after knocking and waiting a moment, opened the door to a dim, red-lit dance studio. His footsteps echoed off harlequin floors as he approached a cushioned armchair with a small notecard reading: *Sit in me*. Brows furrowed, he fell into the comfortable seat. Mirrored walls surrounded him on three sides, with a curtain sectioning the room in half.

Suddenly, a contemporary R&B hit sang out and the curtain spread, exposing a dramatic, spot-lit center pole. As the music built, Morgan stepped into view. Her svelte hourglass figure touched the light, revealing an unexpected ensemble. She resembled an L.A. Kings cheerleader in black and silver booty shorts, a cropped jersey, Kings baseball hat and sky-high black heels. So much for her *born and raised* loyalty to the Anaheim Ducks.

Morgan seized the pole steadily with both hands. Taking several deep breaths, she stared into the mirror behind Chase. Finally, she ascended the pole leisurely, artfully. He clutched the chair armrests, his erection rising. Whatever Chase had expected, it certainly wasn't this.

Reaching the ceiling, she tossed her baseball cap at him before commencing a sensual, acrobatic show. Her curves owned every slide, climb, invert, hang, split and spin. She made the craft appear effortless, though it obviously took skill.

Chase sat slack-jawed, his mighty manhood longing for liberation from snug jeans. Raw pre-cum met his boxers, as though he might bust early, which had never, ever happened. The electrifying visual of Morgan expertly dancing while sporting his favorite team's logo didn't help matters. Ravenous, he watched and waited.

Morgan had discovered pole fitness several years prior, while investigating celebrity fitness regimes. The studio had surprisingly become a second home, her fellow pole sisters a second family. Normally, she and other women practiced in a fun, supportive environment, building muscle and confidence. She'd daydreamed about performing for a man in a far-off, maybe-one-day sort of way.

The music switched to the next song on her *Seductive* playlist, an encouraging mix with songs by strong, successful female performers. After spiraling down the pole, she landed a backward somersault gracefully on her knees and finally met Chase's one-green, one-hazel eyes. Biting a glossed lip, she crawled forward minxlike with wavy, disheveled hair, as though he'd already screwed her senseless.

On her approach, he leaned in for a kiss. But she nudged him back. She'd come too far to relinquish control. Instead, she sat back on her heels. Teasingly, she thrust her hips, lifting the jersey once, twice and over her head to reveal a black rhinestone pushup bra. After tossing the jersey at him, she continued crawling coquettishly, perky cleavage displayed.

Forcing his knees apart, she unzipped and tugged his jeans down along with those infamous BB boxers. She placed the Kings hat backward on her head before her mouth met his throbbing cock. With a pleasurable moan, she devoured its full length. Chase's entire body responded, toes flexing, bum cheeks gripping, mouth tight and trembling. His hands clasped the armrests, struggling to hold back.

Such thirsty, blatant desperation tempted her to rush. Only too well she knew what those masterful hands could do. But Morgan yanked his briefs back up instead.

She stood and kneeled on an armrest before rolling across his lap toward the other armrest. Licking his lips, Chase watched the seductive s-shaped curve where her lower back molded to her behind, which was delightfully outlined in cheeky hip huggers. When he spanked her bottom playfully, she glanced back and shook her head, painted cat-eyes glowering.

Once she shifted to straddle him, her crimson lips trailed his neck and chest. Then she tilted back, unclasped her bra in front and grinded against his lap. Sliding her hands through his ashy blonde locks, she tugged, fending off his attempts to suck her eager, hardening nipples. After removing her bra, she stripped him to the beat, discarding his t-shirt and jeans.

Returning to his lap, she nibbled those tender lips. The heat intensified, their bodies thrusting together in only boxers. Lips on lips. Chest to chest. Wetness seeped through her lingerie as she glided along his solid shaft. A bead of sweat dripped from his forehead to her chest, and he licked it.

After carefully removing his briefs, she slowly stripped hers. He pulled her back onto his lap. Finally, she straddled his tip into her desperate body. He grabbed her waist to enter faster, but she slapped his hands away and glared. Inch by gradual, merciless inch, she took in his broad length. Leaning back, she moaned, hips circling to consume all his enormity. Soon she slowed, weary from the arduous performance.

So he clutched her waist, bobbing her up and down rapidly. Morgan rubbed her clit, something she'd never attempted during sex but which put release in her own hands. And it didn't take long.

"I'm close," she whispered.

"Me too."

They climaxed in precise unison, bodies entwined. "Fuck, Morgan," he growled as she clenched, hugging him tight.

"Fuck," she concluded, eyes lolled in an orgasmic, euphoric daze. Still embraced, they caught labored breaths.

After a moment, Chase held up a sealed chrome condom packet. "We forgot something in the heat of the moment."

Morgan shrugged and stood to wipe herself with a towel. "I've been taking my pills consistently. I'm not worried."

Chase watched her clean up. His films always omitted this step, the messy lovemaking aftermath. Taking the cloth next, he toweled her frothy juices off his pubic hair and asked, "What inspired this show, darling?"

Morgan dressed hastily and explained, "Weeks ago, that day in Venice, you mentioned a desire to relinquish control. After seeing how you've taken care of your mom and your exes, it's no wonder you crave a dominant woman. You need and deserve a break."

He flashed bleached teeth and pulled her into his lap as she continued, "You turned my greatest carnal fantasies into realities, helped me unleash a brazen boldness I'd never known." Her hand met his chest. "You've helped me explore *my* desires, *my* passions. That's what inspired this. As you fulfilled my fantasies, I wanted to fulfill yours."

His heart ballooned into his throat, leaving him speechless. "Thank you," he finally screeched.

"My pleasure." She leaned in, gaze direct. "And yours, I presume."

He nodded, then shook his head. "You know, whenever you mentioned going to fitness class, I assumed spinning or yoga. No wonder you're toned as fuck." His fingers danced along her smooth, stone thighs. "Any other mysteries locked in your vault?"

Crossing her arms, she folded into them, shielding her face. "This might explain some things. Maybe not. I don't know . . ." she mumbled. "My ex was a porn addict. Why I was with him, I can't say. Maybe I hungered for someone, anyone, to explore my sexuality with. Whenever we hooked up, he put on hardcore, degrading porn for us to reenact. He convinced me I was into it, so it seemed like I was exploring my desires too. But we only explored his needs. And I fell for it." Tears welled in her eyes and as one flowed down her cheek, he kissed it.

She continued, "By the end, he'd choke me and call me a whore and I'd come. Over time, it was the only way I could orgasm. I always felt disgusting afterward. There was nothing sexy about being called a whore. Those weren't my desires. One day the spell finally broke and I simply told him, *I don't like this* and left."

Choking and name-calling had never occurred to Chase as problematic. While performing scenes, brutality was usually obligatory. And his exes seemed to enjoy savagery. But if they hadn't, he would have gladly embraced their needs. "I could punch that scumbag in the face!" he snapped. "You should never have had to experience anything like that ever."

Squeezing her tight, he inhaled the vanilla scent that stirred him. He'd uttered the *L* word in past relationships, as an unrequited, safe response to keep exes from whipping plates. Now, his heart swelled with an overwhelming affection unfelt before. Considering life without Morgan made his chest reel. "I love you," he said.

His light kiss evolved into a make-out session, their mouths melding together. Then she withdrew, palmed his chin and met two smitten, compassionate eyes. "I love you, too."

Chapter Fifteen: All Scoops

"Sidney. In here!" Jason exclaimed from his office.

Sean saluted and Morgan bit her lip, unsure what this could be. After that computer virus, she'd compiled another puff piece, investigating the best lubrication method. She and Chase had tested various options and concluded the industry had it right with virgin coconut oil.

"Is this you?" Jason asked as she entered his lair.

Lips curled, she sat, praying he hadn't discovered her Barbie Blue porn cameo.

He jutted his phone forward to present a photo of Morgan staring at a sunflower painting, that day she went roller skating in Venice with Chase.

"Yes," Morgan replied, puzzled. "Where did you find that?"

"After months offline, the Prince of Sin's grand return to social media is a photo of you, captioned *My darling*?"

Though her heart swooned, her stomach sank like it was plunging through quicksand. She nodded, struggling to read his expression and determine the degree of trouble she was in.

"Also, Marcus claims to have seen you here with the Prince after hours . . ." Jason lifted a taped-together, shredded copy of Morgan's cleavage.

Morgan gulped, assuming she was about to get fired.

"Are you fucking him?" Jason asked candidly.

Her eyes widened.

"Shipping, tapping, smushing, swiping . . . whatever you

millennial/Gen Z cusp babies are calling it this week. Sidney, are you *fraternizing* with Chase Prince?"

"We've been hanging out." Mentally, she unpacked her desk, wondering if a laptop and some file folders could fit in one storage box.

"You're shtupping the most famous wang on earth and this is the best you've got?" He slammed her lube script on his desk.

"What?"

"I asked for another feature. If you're in deep with Prince Pecker himself, why the fuck are you vlogging about coconut oil? You have the in. Give me some dirt!"

Jason would never fire her over an affair with a celebrity. Marcus had gotten promoted after pursuing a gay teen sitcom star and then outing him. Jason was all scoops, no ethics.

"I'll post this fluff over the weekend," he said. "But I need something better to run over the holiday."

Jason considered breaking scandals over Christmas vacation a company priority. He wanted people waiting at airports, relaxing beachside, resting in ski chalets or cuddling under mistletoes watching *Slander*'s shocking, revelatory new videos.

"Something better?" she asked.

"The juicier the better."

Blanking on months of notes and research, Morgan simply nodded. She stood to exit as Jason added, "And if you procure my holiday scoop, your new title will be Producer."

Eyes wide with the prospect, she remembered this was Jason. "Could I get that in writing?"

"Find my scoop," Jason insisted, waving her out. "Then we'll talk."

"You should vlog about which porn stars are naturally that massive in real life. I'd gladly assist with some hands-on research," Sean said, falling into hysterics. "How many inches does your Prince flaunt?"

Working in a dark, windowless edit bay with outdated computer monitors and equipment, Morgan scanned clips and flipped through a notepad. Sean styled her hair in a loose bun, fastened it with her old scrunchie, then untied it and commenced a French braid.

"I can't write about Chase anymore," she declared. "It's conflict of interest. There must be something else." Her phone vibrated and they looked down to Mandi's name flashing on-screen.

"Did your famjam see His Highness's post?"

"Shit. I hadn't considered that."

It was unlikely the Prince of Sin's post would reach Morgan's family. They followed hard news, not social feeds.

"You *still* haven't told them?" he asked.

"How do you explain to your family that you're not just dating a porn star but *the* porn star?" Morgan opened Mandi's text message, which stated that she'd be in the neighborhood that week and wanted to meet up. "Weird. The she-devil rarely drives up to L.A."

"Maybe baby sis wants all the lurid deets?"

"Only you're that perverted."

"And don't you forget it!" Sean tied the braid. "B-T-dubs, I need your opinion," nudging Morgan's swivel chair aside, he snatched the mouse and opened a browser. "What do you think of this potensh new roommate for me? I need your help deciding, because major sketchos post online ads."

She jolted at the words *online ads* and flipped through her notebook.

"Sweetums, thoughts?" Sean asked. "Earth to Morgan Sidney!"

Her finger stopped on a page with Kali's name. A wide smile formed.

"What?" he asked.

"I found my feature."

That week, Morgan toiled in the conference room, organizing photos and notes along the table and walls, piecing together her feature story. Since most people left town for Christmas, it was a quiet mid-afternoon at the office on December twenty-third. When her phone rang, she answered it instinctively.

"Really, Morgan? Answering after just one ring?"

Morgan's body and face wilted.

"What if I were a gentleman caller?" Mandi continued. "Don't let prospective suitors know you're desperate."

Morgan side-eyed as Mandi snickered.

"Sup, Mandi?"

"I was in the neighborhood doing some last-minute holiday shopping and stopped by your office."

Morgan's heart pounded as she cracked the door open. Mandi stood at her desk, perfectly coiffed in a beige, knee-length skirt and matching blazer, hands filled with high-end shopping bags.

"Hiding from me? The receptionist mentioned you were here!" Mandi turned a corner toward the edit suites, a shrew on the hunt.

Squaring the door shut, Morgan noted walls adorned with posters of nude porn stars. A doomed prey, she scrambled to tear down evidence of her still-secret, X-rated life.

"Morgan!" Bursting in, Mandi pointed to a photo of au naturel Kali Sensuale and asked, "What's this?"

"Um, it's for a body-positive, love yourself, New Year, New You piece I'm doing," Morgan muttered, quickly grabbing her purse. "You know, be comfortable in your own skin, yadda, yadda. Let's eat." She sped through the doorway.

Mandi gawked at a photo of Tori Jade spread eagle on a

station wagon and followed her sister.

Twenty minutes later, they sat in a nearby patio food court. Ordinarily a midday hub for midtown professionals, it was eerily quiet just before the holidays.

Mandi gobbled cascading nachos. Chunks of guacamole and sour cream plummeted off a chip. "Mmmmm," Mandi cooed, mouth full. "These nachos are *the best!*"

"Don't save me a bite," Morgan uttered, surprised by pregnant Mandi stuffing her face in public like a commoner.

"Really, Morgan? You have your pizza."

"I was kidding."

Not one for chitchat, Mandi jumped to it. "What happened with you and Grant? I hope you didn't wear *that*." She pointed to Morgan's baggy gray sweatshirt.

"Yes, I wore a sweatshirt from high school on a date."

A wad of cheese tumbled out of Mandi's gaping mouth.

"That was sarcasm."

"Why do you even still *own* something from high school?"

"I don't think either of us felt it," Morgan explained slowly, careful not to misspeak and send Mandi into a tizzy. "Grant is very nice. But there wasn't a spark."

"Mmm-hmm," Mandi cooed. "I get that."

"*You* get that?" Morgan couldn't recall a time snide, bitter Mandi got her view on anything. "You were dead-set on me and Grant becoming your and Noah's BFF double-daters."

"Yes, but I understand if Grant didn't stir your loins." Mandi giggled, shaking her torso.

Baffled, Morgan squinted and asked, "So *you* are being considerate of *my loins*?"

"Mmm-hmm. So no to Grant. But you aren't seeing anybody else?"

"Nope," Morgan blurted, ankles crossed and shoulders drawn back.

"I get it," Mandi said. "Taking time for you." Avocado splatted onto her pristine skirt.

Nodding slowly at this imposter, Morgan stood and announced, "I have to pee."

As Morgan rounded a corner, Mandi pounced. She reached for Morgan's purse and removed her phone. Guessing the password, she punched in Morgan's birthdate.

Mandi didn't *happen* to be in Los Angeles. A few days earlier, Grant had mentioned that while he and Morgan had a lovely date, she'd seemed distracted — particularly after spotting flowers from another man at her doorstep.

Quickly scanning recent messages, Mandi stopped at a contact labelled *Darling*. Within seconds, she saved Darling's number in her own phone before returning Morgan's. "No mystery men evade me," she muttered under her breath. "Especially not mystery *darlings*."

On Christmas Eve morning, Chase biked to work. Sober several weeks, he carried extra swagger in his step. Plus, Morgan had agreed to spend Christmas morning with him and Sandra, so he stood on cloud ten.

After parking at the Lit Empire compound, the Prince of Sin strutted through sliding doors to approach Jazmine at the front desk. In red patent, thigh-high boots, Jazmine was not your typical receptionist. Once a porn-player, she didn't look a day under sixty, with wrinkly leather skin, purple hair extensions, huge hoop earrings and a smoker's voice.

"Dah-ling," she rasped. Nobody knew where Jazmine was born. Eastern Europe was a safe bet, perhaps Austria or Hungary, but definitely someplace else. With her on-camera days long gone, Jazmine had run the compound's reception since Chase played in diapers.

He kissed both her cheeks, but she grabbed his face to plant a goopy third on his lips. "You look mah-velous," she said, squeezing his bicep.

"I feel mah-velous. Where am I today, Jazzy?"

"You are in *ze* first Locker Room." She waved him off and took a phone call.

Entering a white corridor, Chase spotted Tori at the opposite end but didn't even flinch at her presence. She strutted like a runty runway model, in a sparkly bandage dress and clunky sky-high wedges.

Approaching Locker Room One, he expected her to pass and asked, "Whose pussy juice will you be guzzling today?" But as he grabbed the doorknob, her hand jutted overtop, dagger nails clenching. With a yelp, he whipped his arm back as she twisted the knob to enter.

Chase sprinted back to Jazmine's desk. "Jazzy, you must have made a mistake. Where am I supposed to be?"

"I tell you already. Locker Room One," Jazmine reiterated, "with Madame Jade-Empress."

His face whitened. Picking his cuticles, he returned to set. Tori awaited his return with crossed arms. Stepping inside, he asked, "Since when were you released to do boy-girl scenes again?"

"I do what I please," she squeaked, shoving the door closed so vigorously it nearly smacked him. He glared, longing to tear that garish tiara from her blonde extension bird's nest and break it in half.

A pimply, spectacled teenager passed and Chase demanded, "Whose set is this?"

The kid shrugged and continued unraveling lighting cords. Looking around, Chase spotted the director, a cranky Bostonian he'd worked with before. Marching over, he spewed, "Who booked me with Tori?"

"Came from upstairs," the director said, chomping gum and fiddling with a camera.

"Tori's master orchestrated this?" Chase asked doubtfully.

"I need to talk to Viola."

"She's not here," he grumbled. "It's Christmas."

Chase side-eyed him and smirked, reminded of Morgan and how crushed she'd be if he performed this scene.

The director took a phone call, so Chase marched to Tori. She eyed him through the vanity mirror while fixing her make-up. "Why the long face, babe?"

"Tor, I'm not doing this."

"It's on the schedule, so it's happening." She swiveled in her stool and stood to face him. "As if you aren't itching to munch my taco."

He audibly gagged.

"What? You'd rather go balls-deep into your *Slander whore*?"

That word from Tori's mouth seemed so vulgar to him now. "Don't call her that."

"Why not? The *whore* doesn't like it?"

"Stop everything!" the director shouted. "We're on hold."

"What?" Tori barked. She whipped around so sharply her tiara escaped and smacked the teenager's face.

"Lee Lyla's test came back positive," he explained. "We're on a moratorium."

When a performer's STD test results came back positive, production stopped until anyone who'd slept with that person since their last test got rechecked and cleared. Chase had gotten with Lee Lyla recently. He opened his phone calendar to check the exact date, but the director answered for him. "You're first generation, Prince. Go get tested."

Brows raised, Chase shot his ex a cocksure smirk. Never had he been so relieved to possibly have the clap. Since most porn holds were from false positives, he wasn't concerned. They were more of a bitch than a scare. He'd lose a few days of work and had to get tested but was saved by the bell.

"This is not over!" Tori shouted, strumming catty nails on

her hips as Chase swiftly exited. He dialed Benny's number.

"Kid, I just heard," Benny fired. "You at a clinic? Don't worry. I'm sure it's nothing."

"Why the fuck was I booked with Tori?" Chase shoved open a back-exit door and burst into an alleyway.

"Tori? What? I thought this was about—"

"I'm currently storming off set, where my skank ex stood eager to bob on my cock."

"It must have been a mistake. That new intern, in our office . . ."

"Benny, I've been with you since day one, but I don't need you."

"Chase, Bubelah, Motek . . ." Benny stammered. "Whoever scheduled this is will leave the Benny Solomon Agency with my leather boot imprint on their ass. This will never happen again!"

"Better not." Chase disconnected and vaulted onto his motorcycle. But seconds later the phone rang. "What?" he roared.

"Hi there," said a perky, unrecognizable female voice.

If his number had been leaked again, he would lose it. "Who is this?"

Chapter Sixteen: The Mystery Guest

The Sidneys were not very religious. Al was raised by Catholic by Italian immigrant parents. His father died when he was young, leaving his mother too busy rearing him and his sister to prioritize church. A devout Christian in her youth, Kaya Sidney let her worshiping ways wane over time. Growing up, Morgan and Mandi occasionally went to chapel with their grandparents. But Al and Kaya prioritized family customs and traditions instead of God, so holiday celebrations at Casa Sidney were consistently smashing.

Christmas took the candy cane cake. On the Saddleback slope foothills, the Sidney's backyard overlooked cookie-cutter Orange County subdivisions. But despite mid-sixties temperatures and breathtaking views of an idyllic purple, orange and yellow southern California sunset, no one had to dream of a white Christmas. Sleeted artificial snow coated the back lawn, patio and awning, surrounding a swimming pool and hot tub. The large backyard evergreen had been decorated with heirloom ornaments from across the globe. And bright colored lights spiraled around pillars and the fence.

More than just festive décor, a jolly atmosphere welcomed dozens of guests, from Kaya's parents to cousins and family friends. Even the Goldberg family attended, providing latkes with sour cream and applesauce. Children frolicked, whipped snowballs at each other and splashed into a steaming hot tub. Adults sipped cocktails and noshed on a decadent buffet as peppermint, apple cider and roast turkey aromas swept the yard.

Seated on a lounge chair, Morgan caught up with her grandmother, a tinier, seventy-something version of Kaya and Mandi. Generosa, the Sidney's longtime housekeeper, refilled their eggnog mugs. "Yes, Grandma, *fleek* is no longer *on fleek*," Morgan explained. Grandma cherished being in-the-know. *Hip, even without a real hip,* as she proudly asserted.

"You know, dear, I stay up-to-date with *Slander*. I watch videos of those ludicrous housewives and follow the rapper diss track wars . . ."

As grandma opined about youngsters today, Morgan took a deep, relaxed breath. Holidays warmed her soul. Wishing Chase could meet all these loved ones, she pictured him strolling in sporting a crisp, two-toned button-up under his leather jacket and . . . Morgan froze. She was either eggnog wasted or the Prince of Sin had just moseyed through a side gate.

Leaning back, she twisted her neck and plopped oafishly backward, pounding the brick patio. Eggnog flew, just missing her festive red dress.

"Oh my!" Grandma clamored.

A small crowd gathered and a family friend helped Morgan stand. She quickly composed herself and scurried across the yard, yanking Chase to a secluded pathway before anybody could spot him.

"Smooth landing," he said before pecking her lips. "Are you OK?"

"Hi," she chirped, masking confusion and hesitation about how exactly he'd appeared at her family's holiday shebang.

"Sorry I'm late. Your sister said four, but . . . Do your parents drink whiskey? I hope so." He glanced down, shuffling a bottle between hands.

Her fists curled as she realized this was Mandi's stunt. But Chase seemed nervous, so she played along. "I'm stoked you're here," she said. Pressing glossed lips to his smooth ones, she paused to think, then pulled back. "But I must confess, I'm not ready to tell my family about your . . . career. Could we leave that tiny detail out?"

"So you're asking me to lie to your family?"

As his eyes lowered, her heart sank. "Not lie. Maybe say you're an actor and leave it at that." She squeezed his fidgety hand and mimicked that mopey, imploring look he once used while asking her to pull his quote. "Please? I beg, I plead."

"Ech. Do guys actually fall for that?" But he half-smiled his resignation, emerald eyes flickering in the setting sun's final rays.

"I love you," she said.

After kissing her forehead, he said, "I love you too."

Hand-in-hand they entered the backyard. "Say hello to the North Pole of SoCal," Morgan welcomed. He crouched down, excitedly packing a snowball.

"Helllllooooooooo!" Mandi cooed across the deck, gallivanting over with an exaggerated sheer green shawl fluttering. She squeezed Chase into the most extravagant hug she'd ever given, her tiny baby bump protruding into his thigh. Over Mandi's shoulder, Chase squashed the snowball playfully against Morgan's head.

"So nice to finally meet your *darling*," Mandi said, pulling away to shoot Morgan a snarky sneer.

"Who's this?" Kaya chimed, rushing up.

"Mother, this is the mystery guest," Mandi explained. "Morgan's secret new beau."

Kaya whooped delightedly, embracing Chase. Al approached next, statuesque and stern, especially compared to his overly enthusiastic wife and daughter. Morgan held her breath.

"Daddy, this is . . ." Mandi began, trailing off.

"Harrison," Chase revealed, extending a hand. "Krol."

With a firm shake, Al nodded. His face remained hard, but

the gesture was enough for Morgan to exhale.

"Morgan, he is to die for," Kaya whispered, ogling Chase.

"For you both," Chase said, handing the fine whiskey bottle to Al. "Thank you for having me, Mr. and Mrs. Sidney."

Kaya laughed heartily. "No, no, just Kaya." Squeezing his arm, she tugged him. "Come, come, you must meet the whole gang." Al followed as Kaya led Chase toward a large group.

"Really Morgan?" Mandi hissed. "Lying to me about your dating life? Grant mentioned you might be canoodling someone else, so I investigated." Mandi tapped Morgan's phone, huffed and joined the small crowd.

Morgan smirked, grateful her sister made a mediocre investigator and remained seemingly unaware of Harrison's second identity. Watching Kaya flaunt him, she just hoped nobody else would discern that Harrison Krol was actually . . .

"Holy crap!" Noah bellowed, carrying a tray of pigs in a blanket through an open sliding glass door. "Isn't that the Prince of —"

Morgan clutched Noah's forearm, nearly tipping the tray, and snapped, "No! He is most definitely not the Prince of anything. Tonight, he's Harrison Krol. Just a guy I'm going with."

"Ha! Pretty sure everyone with Wi-Fi is *going* with that guy."

Her grip tightened. "If you expose him, everyone will know you're a smut-savorer." They both knew Mandi would go ballistic.

"Okay, okay." Freeing his arm, Noah stepped forward. "Let's meet your new man, baby sis!" Noah strode toward the group with Morgan hot on his tail. He smacked Chase's back heartily. "Great to meet you, friend." Presenting the tray, he grinned so wide his face looked like it could split in two. "Have a cocktail weenie. They're fit for a king, or at the very least, a *prince*."

Morgan shot Noah a threatening stare as Mandi snatched the tray and picked at some weenies. "Harrison was just explaining life as a Hollywood actor," Mandi explained, then scoffed. "Can you imagine, dear? Our Morgan, dating a performer." She shoveled two hot dogs into her mouth.

"Sounds like a *hard* line of work," Noah replied, nudging Morgan.

Chase detailed his Mr. Banana Package shoot to the group, elaborating on a monkey that squished a banana on his head. Everyone fell into hysterics. Morgan beamed, noting how naturally her prince eased from bundle of nerves back to charming.

"Would we have seen you in anything?" Toby Goldberg piped in.

"Yes, have we?" Noah added. "Weren't you on that royal family drama?"

Morgan pressed her shoe on Noah's toe.

"Ouch!"

"What?" Mandi snapped through a mouthful of appetizers.

"Uh, mosquito bit me," Noah lied, rubbing his shoulder.

"I doubt you'd recognize me from anything," Chase said, turning to Toby. "My work is low budget, indie stuff." He wrapped an arm around Morgan's waist and she softened, finally loosening. Al's graying brows furrowed. "But Morg has me considering directing."

"Harrison, you look *too* familiar," Kaya said, leaning forward to scrutinize his face.

"I'm certain we've met before," Toby said. "Does your family winter in Aspen?"

Chase shrugged as Noah commented, "Seems more like a *Mammoth* guy to me." Then he whispered to Morgan, "Imagine these soccer moms catching a Chase Prince matinee." She smacked Noah's arm and he yelped, jolting. "Damned mosquitos are really at it tonight."

Mandi scowled and barked, "What mosquitos? It's winter."

"Sweetie, perhaps I know your Mother from the country club?" Kaya asked, examining him. "Your face is so familiar, but bless my soul if I can place it."

"He's from L.A.," Morgan said. "You wouldn't know his family."

"Rosa, come meet Morgan's gorgeous new sweetheart." Kaya squeezed Chase's bicep and giggled.

"OK!" Generosa cried while refilling a champagne glass. She turned and, spotting Chase, dropped the bottle. Glass shattered on the deck. "Dios mios!" She rambled in Spanish, ignoring sharp, scattered shards threatening their feet.

"What on earth is she babbling about?" Kaya asked, turning to bilingual Noah.

"She's . . ." he began.

Morgan gulped.

" . . . impressed!" Noah continued. "Harrison starred on one of her Spanish telenovas. Come, Rosa. Let's get a broom." As Noah guided flabbergasted Generosa inside, he shot Morgan a discreet thumbs up.

"Must have been quite a role," Kaya said.

Changing the subject, Morgan turned to Al. "Dad, Chase was raised by a single Mother, too."

"Who's Chase?" Mandi snapped.

Frozen, Morgan felt her world cave in, until . . .

"My dog," Chase answered. "My Mom raised me and the pup herself."

Once Al nodded impassively, Morgan exhaled.

Chase winked covertly at Morgan before facing Al, "Mr. Sidney, I recently read your editorial comparing single parents of baby boomers with single parents of millennials. It was quite a read."

Al hummed.

"Your take on minimum wage was interesting," he continued. "Though with millennials, you conveniently skimmed past low-income families."

Friends and family stared aghast. Everyone knew Al Sidney's critics better be prepared to support their arguments. "Understandable," Al said.

Several jaws fell.

"It's tough remembering life in the gutter once you've moved onto caviar," Chase said, lifting his fish egg snack. "No disrespect, but even for myself. Even with my minor success, I often forget why I crossed into my line of work. To support my mother."

Al studied him, then said, "Tell me more. Over a drink. Scotch?" His eyes flashed toward the bar.

"I'm more of a whiskey man," Chase responded, following Al.

Kaya and Morgan exchanged intrigued glances while Mandi pouted, duck faced.

By midnight, only Chase, Morgan, Mandi and Noah remained, huddled around a fire pit sipping cocoa with Kaya and Al. Chase fed Morgan a roasted marshmallow, both giggling as it oozed onto her nose and chin.

"It means everything that you wanted me here," Chase told Morgan privately. "Sorry again for being late. I had to get—" But he stopped. Mentioning the production hold would only worry her, especially since they'd recently made love without a condom. He decided to wait until his results came back before saying anything—they just couldn't be intimate until then.

"Don't apologize," she said. "I'm just glad you made it."

Al and Chase continued their ongoing dialogue. After

dissecting specific pieces of Al's work, Chase had inquired about Al's most memorable experiences in the field. He hung on, enthralled as Al detailed sneaking to Woodstock for his high school newspaper and covering the Munich massacre in college. Chase also observed Morgan's animated chat with Kaya and conjured images of creating their own family someday.

Behind them, Generosa cleared trays and blabbered on the phone. "Si, si, estrella del porno. El Príncipe!"

"You kids can head to bed," Kaya insisted, standing. "We'll help Rosa clear up."

Everyone said goodbye. Extending a haughty cheek kiss to Chase, Mandi declared, "It was *so* nice to meet you, Harrison. See, Morgan, even though I invited him behind your back, Harrison had a fabulous time."

Chase nodded impassively, masking disappointment. Morgan mouthed *Sorry*, but he stared down at his scuffed up boat shoes, feeling like a drifter crashing cotillion. "I should head home."

"Harrison, don't be silly. You'll sleep in our guestroom!" Kaya insisted. "It's much too late to venture up the 405."

"I had such a nice time," he said, grabbing his jacket. "But I'm meeting my mom early tomorrow." He hugged Kaya, who squeezed tightly, then shook Al's hand. "Thank you for your kind hospitality."

Morgan placed a remorseful hand over his chest and said, "I'll drive up before lunch."

Chase nodded, pecked her cheek and exited the yard.

As she hugged Morgan, Mandi muttered, "He may have won Daddy over. But really, an *actor*? How gauche. Grant is more your type. And status."

"Grant is more *your* type and status," Morgan clarified.

Noah patted Morgan's back and nodded his big bro approval. "I like the guy."

Mandi snorted. "Time to go." He followed her outside.

"Harrison is quite the sweetheart," Kaya stated, fluffing throw pillows.

"He's a bright young man," Al said, squeezing Morgan's shoulders from behind.

As Morgan heard Chase's bike rev, various emotions pooled — relief Chase's identity remained undisclosed, proud he had survived and impressed Al, but mostly disappointment in herself, for not inviting him.

Morgan woke early and trekked north to the South L.A. address Chase had texted. She parked on a side street and followed a weedy walkway to a rundown building. Approaching a locked door, she knocked and waited. A hunched elderly woman cracked it open and peeked out. "Yes?"

"I'm . . ." Morgan trailed, not sure where she was. "Are the Krols here?"

A chain unhooked and the lady opened the squeaky door. "Come on in, doll."

Morgan followed her to a cafeteria with low ceilings, where thin curtains covered sooty windows. Women and young children wearing dated clothes ate at two long tables. Behind a serving counter, Sandra wore a smock and her long, gray locks confined under a hairnet. She doled out mashed potatoes and, spotting Morgan, nodded.

"Darling." Chase approached from behind.

Turning around, Morgan examined his white smock and gold-streaked hair, also held by mesh. "You spend Christmas at a women's shelter?"

"Every year." He kissed her and offered a ruffled apron. "I need an assistant for my baking class, you game?"

While Sandra led an employment seminar titled *Sell Your Skills*, Chase and Morgan entertained a dozen youngsters in the kitchen. Flour puffs soared as the children poured and stirred ingredients, following Morgan and Chase's directions. Morgan struggled not to laugh when CiCi, an adorable five-year-old in pigtails, bawled because an eggshell landed in her bowl. Removing it, Morgan cracked jokes to calm her.

"How long have you volunteered here?" Morgan asked while distributing holiday-themed cookie cutters.

"Since we got out. We lived here the first year of my life. And return to volunteer each year. You're the first person I've ever brought, though." As his fingers entwined with hers, she squeezed tight.

Later, the children washed sprinkles and icing off their hands and faces before heading elsewhere for naptime. CiCi brought Chase a plate of heart-shaped sugar cookies and said, "These are from her." She pointed to Morgan, giggled and scurried to exit.

The plate contained five cookies, with S, O, R, R, Y written in icing. "For what, my sexily disheveled sous-chef?" he asked.

"Not inviting you yesterday," she said. "I'm so glad you came."

Chase removed her hairnet, smoothed a few flyaway hairs and said, "Even though you didn't invite me, you still let me in." He leaned close to suck her lower lip before she could reach his. Their mouths wrestled a minute.

Pulling back, she joked, "We should name our firstborn in CiCi's honor."

"You can name our children whatever you please," he said.

"Give me ten years. I still have a world to change, remember?"

Chase beamed proudly as Sandra peeked in. "How did things go in here?"

"Great," Morgan responded. "Those kids are adorable. Did your seminar go well?"

"I hope it proved advantageous. But you never know until

your pupils enter the world and make change happen for themselves."

Morgan nodded. "Do you exchange gifts?"

"Not really," Chase responded.

"Well, I didn't know, so . . ." Morgan handed him a red envelope. He removed a card with a receipt for a cinematography class. "You're registered for winter session. No more excuses. I *know* you'll be an amazing director."

"Wow," Chase responded sincerely. He'd researched film classes but never had the courage to sign up. "What a thoughtful gift."

Sandra beamed off Chase's elation.

"And . . ." Morgan handed Sandra a sketch of two hands fondling a curvy woman from behind. "An artist friend sent it from Italy." Sandra admired the illustration.

After untying her apron, Morgan washed her hands. "I should get going." She extended a hand to Sandra, who pulled her into a polite hug. Morgan's brows lifted as she patted Sandra's back.

"Such thoughtful gifts," Sandra commended, pulling away. "I am quite pleased you joined us today."

Chase swooped in next to softly smooch Morgan's lips.

"Thank you for inviting me, darling," Morgan said. "And letting me in." With a polished wink, she left.

"Morgan might be growing on me, baby," Sandra admitted, rubbing his back.

He grinned. She'd been growing on him for some time. Pulling out his phone, he texted her: *For your Xmas gift I.O.U. one final fantasy. Let's ring in the new year with a BANG (wink wink)*

CHAPTER SEVENTEEN: THE NOT-SO-CALM BEFORE

Studio City, a San Fernando Valley neighborhood just north of Los Angeles, boasted many mainstream TV and film studios. But it also harbored Whiskey Pins, host to a monthly porn star bowling and karaoke night. Whenever conventional media covered this not-so-secret dive bar frequented by carnal VIPs, civilian fans flooded it for a month or two. Eventually the event faded back into oblivion for most. But it remained a hotspot for industry folk from washed up has-beens to anal all-stars.

Morgan parked in a considerably vacant mini-mall parking lot. She'd heard Whiskey Pins was *the* porn star scene, though wedged between a supermarket and beauty salon, it hardly seemed scandalous. But music and laughter blared inside. If only the suburban housewives buying groceries knew who downed drafts next door.

She entered a congested sports bar with low ceilings hovered over crowded red booths. Rumbling bowling balls and toppling pins from a dozen crowded lanes disrupted three dorky dudes singing Backstreet Boys on a tiny dance floor. Despite text posted on various screens, they somehow managed to botch the lyrics.

Patrons filled tables, though Morgan didn't recognize anybody. Just as she worried it might be a flop, she spotted Tiger Trece with some uberboob babes. He waved, and as she gestured back, her phone buzzed. *Running late, legs*, read Kali

Sensuale's text. Morgan shrugged and approached Tiger's group.

"You stalking me, baby?" Tiger asked as she took the only empty seat. He kissed her cheeks and extended an ebony goddess's hand. The thirty-something woman donned a shimmering forehead band atop endless cascading black curls. "My wife, Iana Rose."

From her research, Morgan recognized Iana as one of porn's most-searched females. Not sure what to do with Iana's hand, she gave an awkward shake. "Morgan Sidney."

Iana barely nodded, leering with a distrustful, *what do you want with my husband?* grimace. The boyband wannabes finished and tipped their dollar store top hats. "I'm up next," Tiger boasted, pouring Morgan a glass of cheap beer.

"Maybe I should sign Kali up," Morgan considered aloud.

"Sensuale? Good luck, baby," Tiger said. "Kali sucks cock, the girl don't sing."

Thirty minutes later, still waiting on Kali, an irritated Morgan added Kali's name to the list. Seemingly on cue, Kali Sensuale strutted in as Morgan returned to the table.

She approached in a flared denim mini skirt and five-inch heels. Parking on Morgan's lap, Kali ignored several colleagues attempting to greet her. "This is where you invite me to talk? I hate half these beetches." She ordered a bottle of Chianti and moved to a small booth that opened up. Morgan followed. Behind them, Martini McPie belted a Spice Girls classic with other barely-legal pals.

"Thank you for meeting me," Morgan said professionally, retrieving a notebook. "Have you given more thought to my story? I can show you what I've composed so far. It's almost there, but could use a few more quotes . . ."

"No, no," Kali said. "My life is private. I hate when everybody knows my business."

"Thousands of random people watch you do your business

online!"

"Randoms may watch me, hiding behind little computer screens. But when I go in front of a camera, it is just for me."

Morgan jotted the quote but wouldn't use it without Kali's blessing. The server brought Kali her wine. She chugged a glass before pouring another.

Music faded and a lanky, energetic emcee sporting lips painted tomato red and a cowgirl hat took center floor. "Next up," she declared into a microphone. "An extremely rare, first-time performance by ravishing seductress, Miss Kali Sensuale."

The crowd roared, particularly Tiger's section. Kali had never performed at Whiskey Pins. Nobody could believe it, especially Kali, scowling so distinctly that steam might as well have been spraying out her ears.

"For being late," Morgan explained, smirking mischievously.

"No, no, legs," Kali asserted. "Neanche per sogno!" She stood to exit, but the emcee grasped Kali's hands and tugged her toward the floor.

Kali death-stared Morgan, who remorsefully linked Kali's arm and joined her. "Ignore the crowd," Morgan offered. "Pretend there's a camera. It's just for you."

The lights dimmed, someone handed them microphones and *Independent Women* by Destiny's Child started playing. As Kali stepped back, Morgan croaked the introduction and babbled the first verse despite boos and howling laughter. The crowd didn't care for some nameless nobody. It craved smut sensation Kali Sensuale.

Mortified, Kali watched her friend's ghastly performance. To rescue her, Kali stepped forward as the ballad climbed. She belted the chorus with a surprisingly sensual throaty singing voice. The audience roared as she goofily acted each line. Morgan copied her motions and everyone clapped to the beat.

As the music faded, Kali's smile brightened and the duo bowed to a cheering audience. Dashing outside, they settled on a nearby curb. Kali lit a skinny cigarette and admitted, "Okay, this was fun." For a moment they sat silently, taking in a Queen song playing inside. "You know, legs, I will do it."

"Another song?"

Kali chuckled, exhaling a smoke cloud. "Idiota," she chided. "The story! So long as you don't use my name. Keep me anonimo."

"Anonymous?"

"Sì. If you keep me anonymous, you can tell my story."

Morgan perked upright and grabbed her notebook.

"Ask me your questions now," Kali continued. "So I can go home to sleep. Tomorrow I go back to work."

"You took time off for the holidays?"

"We all took time off, for the hold," Kali explained.

"What hold?"

The next day, Morgan awoke feeling as foolish as when Kali had explained what a production hold meant. After learning Chase had withheld a serious secret that involved her health, Morgan had distractedly carried out Kali's interview. She'd obtained the authentic quotes necessary to complete an epic feature and after leaving Whiskey Pins, pieced Kali's words into the story anonymously and submitted the assignment.

Now, hidden under her alpaca blanket, she dreaded facing a new day. Her mind and body were too exhausted to process everything and too anguished to confront the Prince of Sin. But eventually she rose and drove to the Lit Empire complex, where production was back in swing after Lee Lyla's false positive test.

Lit Empire's studio space was the conglomerate to Jimmy's homey mom 'n pop. Morgan smiled at a security guard and passed through sliding doors into a bright, white lobby with no seating.

She approached Jazmine's desk, where the woman sat reading a gossip magazine. "I'm here for Chase Prince." Morgan extended her media badge. "With *Slander*. He left his wallet at our office."

"Office One," the wrinkly woman responded. Without glancing up, she handed over a photocopied map.

"Thanks." Morgan crossed another set of sliding doors and studied the detailed map. Her vision blurred trying to sort out the compound's numerous sets, each a separate, private studio. Like Jimmy's, it offered stage, gym, bedroom and street sets, but multiples of each, plus offices, theaters, dungeons, dining rooms and a glory hole/adult video store stage. Rates were listed to rent studios for workshops or personal use.

Heading up two stairwells and down a dreary hallway, she passed a mohawked performer wearing a tight leather getup with spiky metal jewelry. Her black-lined eyes evaluated Morgan's skinny jeans, cashmere sweater and plaid headband.

Reaching Office One, Morgan opened a door and entered a huge imitation office with high ceilings and bright lights. Empress Tori Jade-Emperor immediately captured Morgan's attention, slouched topless beside a dated desktop computer, legs-spread in a skimpy businesswoman skirt. *Click. Flash.* A director stood on a platform, snapping still shots of Tori's bare pussy as she gnawed on Chase Prince's big, black scepter. *Click. Flash.*

Spotting Morgan, she jumped up and hurried over.

"I must be on the wrong set," Morgan mumbled, turning to leave.

"Are you here to interview us?" Tori asked, fluttering embellished, curled lashes.

"Interview you? For what?"

"Our comeback scene, silly." Tori shook flawlessly teased

golden hair and extended her sparkly cell phone. "Would you mind snapping a couple shots? My fans are *dying* for a reunion sneak peek."

"What reunion?" Morgan's stomach swirled.

"Mine and Chase's, obvi."

White walls spun as Morgan attempted to steady her legs. She told herself Tori had to be bullshitting—that Chase would never reunite with his ex, on an office set of all places.

Tori clasped Morgan's arm. "Omigod, did he not tell you?"

Morgan whipped her arm free and took a deep breath.

Feigning innocence, Tori beamed. "Thought you could keep the Prince and Princess apart? That's not how happily ever after works."

"But he said you'd never work together . . ." Morgan trailed, realizing if he'd lied about the porn hold, he could also lie about a secret reunion.

Tori inched closer. "Promises from porn stars are meaningless. Pretty sure you're too PG for him. Our sultry sinner likes girls he can treat like *whores*. He mentioned you aren't into that."

Morgan's throat closed. *Inhale. Exhale.* But the pursed-lip breathing wasn't working, so she burst out the doorway and sprinted up one corridor, then another. The hallways became white labyrinths, she a helpless lab rat in Chase Prince's civilian dating experiment.

Finally, she surged down an exit stairwell, nearly tumbling over her feet. Gasping for air, she dashed outside and hurried around the building to her car. She fumbled with keys, unlocked the door and slipped inside. Finding her breath, Morgan sparked the engine as tears formed.

Phone to his ear, Chase exited the restroom as the main studio door crashed shut. "Who was that?" he asked Tori, marching over, nostrils flaring.

"Nobody," she replied, spinning on stilettoed heels.

Into his phone, he roared, "Just deal with it!" and disconnected from Benny, who had again vowed to sort things out. Looking to Tori, he asked, "Who just left?"

"Your whore." Tori giggled.

His body tensed. "Morgan?"

Tori avoided eye contact.

"Seriously?" he croaked, hoping it wasn't true. "What did you say?"

"Chill. I just explained that we're shooting our comeback scene."

"*We* aren't shooting anything!" He threw his hands up. "You dumped me! I dictate my life and career now. You've lost those privileges you lonely, miserable, evil cunt."

Lips pursed, Tori leaned in and scratched down his chest. "You're under contract. And we have a scene to shoot." She pranced to the office chair and hiked her skirt as the annoyed director tapped his toe impatiently. *Click. Flash.*

CHAPTER EIGHTEEN: THE STORM

The studio door flung open so abruptly its knob pierced the plaster wall. Everybody stared as Viola Emperor strode in, overbearingly tall and wearing a long purple cape sweater. "What is this?"

"Master!" Tori gasped. "I thought you were —"

"Thought I was what? Stupid?" Viola scoffed. "My eyes and ears linger everywhere."

"I'm so ashamed!" Tori whined, rushing over.

"Beg forgiveness, my pet!" Viola ordered, strumming black matte fingernails under Tori's chin. Tori kneeled obediently, hugged Viola's leg and nuzzled against it like a docile puppy. Viola smoothed her hair. "Good girl. But you'll still be punished for such naughty behavior." She yanked Tori's blonde locks.

"Thank you, sir," Tori replied.

Their kinky PDA didn't shock or upset Chase, who unexpectedly beamed, glad Tori had found a master to fulfil her needs.

"Get out of here, people!" Viola announced. "I'm cancelling this scene."

Seated at the craft services table, Chase stood and turned to leave. He wanted to find Morgan ASAP, to explain. But Viola's arm halted him. "How dare you seduce *my* bitch? You're done at my Lit Empire. Forever!"

"Oh, well," Chase said with a shrug. Amidst a twelve-year career, he'd never regarded anything work-related as, *Oh, well*. Since meeting Morgan, however, he had been less enthused about performing. Perhaps he would finally quit skating down that endless river. "I don't have time for you, Viola," he spewed, desperate to find Morgan.

"You'll never perform again!" she shouted.

With a brusque wave he exited, elated by the potential his newfound attitude might procure. Rushing outside and toward his motorcycle, he dialed Morgan, but she rejected the call after one ring. "Fuck!" He kicked a tire, hopped on and sped toward her apartment, weaving through traffic. He sprinted upstairs and banged on the door, shouting her name.

A neighbor peeked out. "Shut up!" she shouted. "My toddler's napping!" When she slammed the door, Chase gave a peeved side-eye, which only reminded him of Morgan. Leaning against a wall, he slid to the floor and redialed. This time it went straight to voicemail.

His body curled into fetal position. But then, eyes illuminated, he scrolled to Morgan's anti-theft app. Staring at it, he paused, feeling shifty. With a light tap, a map opened, pinpointing her phone's location, moving south toward Orange County. He hurried to his motorcycle.

"Hello?" Morgan called out, cracking the front door open to enter Al and Kaya's house. Since she didn't know how to explain her distress without revealing Harrison's true identity, she hesitantly considered finally divulging everything.

Morgan peered into each silent room. When a floorboard squeaked above, she hurried upstairs to Al's study. She entered to Mandi and Al seated in front of a computer monitor. Kaya stood behind, massaging Al's neck.

"Hey!" Morgan faked a smile and rubbed her nose, an attempt to hide her blotchy, post-cry face. But six bulging eyes rose aghast. Confused, she rounded the desk. Onscreen rested a paused image of Barbie Blue standing in the alley outside Club XXX.

As Chase weaved through southbound traffic en route to Orange County, his helmet Bluetooth dinged. He connected the call. "Where are you?" Kali asked immediately, sounding muffled and crackly, as though she were heaving through tears. Chase figured the speakers were defective since Kali never cried.

"Heading to Orange County to find Morgan," he responded. "There was a mix-up and — "

"You have watched her newest story?" Kali asked before sobbing unmistakably.

He realized the speakers worked fine. "Not yet. Why?"

"Go look." She disconnected.

Chase pulled to the shoulder to retrieve his phone. Cars whooshed by as Barbie Blue's most recent *Slander* post loaded. The three-minute piece explored how and why female porn stars entered the industry — through sketchy online ads, desperate for cash or stardom, to live out unsavory fantasies and such. It seemed somewhat accurate, so he wasn't sure what made Kali so upset.

Until two minutes in, when Kali Sensuale was named as a desperate performer who embarked on porn through a shady internet ad. Chase's heart broke, since Kali hated media attention and had matured immensely since her gloomy smut debut. He knew instantly Kali wouldn't have agreed to such a revealing piece and, annoyed Morgan had done something so disrespectful, drove off to console his friend.

"It's abominable," Mandi sobbed into a monogrammed tissue, seated beside Al on the beige living room sofa. Morgan sat uneasily on a matching armchair with Kaya nearby on a soft mint chaise lounge. "The tennis instructor asked if my sister performed pornography now. Imagine my humiliation. Finding out in such a manner. At the club, no less?"

"With global warming, poverty, malnourished children . . . This is hardly the worst problem in the world," Morgan defended.

"Really, Morgan? Shifting to starving kids in Africa? My world has more than caved in. Who knows if they will renew our membership now?"

Morgan side-eyed her.

"Oh please, Mandi," Kaya said.

"Mother, your daughter is a pornographist!" Snot drizzled out her nose as she bawled.

"As long as you pay your club dues, I'm sure they will merrily maintain your and Noah's membership. I'm more concerned about Morgan's wellbeing." Kaya turned toward Morgan. "Is this the only *performance* you engaged in?"

"That's it. A tiny walk-on role with no nudity. And it was for a story!"

"Yes, we saw your *Slander* pieces. Are you covering pornography now?"

"I handed in my final assignment last night."

"Good. That industry seems a bit nutty," Kaya said.

"Nutty? More like slutty!" Mandi bellowed. "Mother, how are you indulging this? She disgraced us!"

"No one's disgraced," Kaya said. "You care too much about everybody else's opinion."

Mandi sobbed. Kaya turned back to Morgan. "So, now we know who Harrison, or, *Chase* is."

Morgan had dreaded this conversation, though she hadn't expected Kaya's calm amenability.

"You are using protection, right? Apparently that industry has had outbreaks of sexually transmitted diseases. Why just last week, I heard —"

"Mother!" Mandi, crying piously, stood and stormed through the foyer. She slammed the front door, dashed to her car and left.

"Don't worry Mom, we're being cautious." Morgan couldn't believe Kaya's primary concern was STDs. Kaya nodded approvingly as Morgan turned to a seemingly somber Al. "Dad?"

"I am not sure what to say," Al replied, standing. "You lied to me, to us." He exited.

"He'll come around," Kaya insisted, rushing over for a hug.

"Maybe," Morgan said, staring at the traditional handwoven area rug. "I'm going to head home."

"Are you sure? It's pitch-black out. Spend the night."

"Thanks. But I'd rather be alone."

After comforting Kali, Chase sweat his anger out for several grueling hours at the gym. The following morning, he jogged around endless holiday tourists at Venice boardwalk, contemplating his New Year's options.

Weeks earlier, Chase had placed New Year's Eve dinner reservations at a trendy Hollywood share plates bistro. And he'd booked a fancy hotel suite, hoping to finally explore Morgan's third fantasy.

How quickly everything had flipped upside down. He and Morgan hadn't spoken in two days. And Chase didn't even know the details of her final fantasy or whether she cared to fulfill it with him anymore.

So unimpressed by Morgan's audacity, he considered ditching their plans to squeeze in another workout. Since Viola's official edict terminating his career at Lit Empire, whipping into tiptop form to book gigs with different companies seemed vital.

Morgan tapped her toe in the stuffy ride share, mentally rehearsing a speech. Chase had initially requested they meet at Jimmy's downtown studio for their New Year's Eve plans, but her sole rendezvous intention was to terminate their relationship. Incensed as she was, Morgan did have some concerns—like whether or not saying adios to Chase meant renouncing her newfound emboldened, confident vixen side.

Dressed to kill—or severely slay, at the very least—Morgan wore a sultry shimmering slinky silver dress with pointed-toe metallic pumps and long threaded earrings. Loose waves framed her naturally made-up face and a vivid purple lip completed the glam look. If all went to plan, she looked hot enough to cut the line at whichever New Year's party Sean had swindled into.

Exiting half a block away, she strutted toward Jimmy's studio, heels clanking and wishing she'd worn more fabric in that part of town. Rounding a corner, she recognized Chase resting against a brick wall in his leather jacket, black slacks and a collared charcoal gray button up.

She stopped to examine him. From afar he embodied seductive mystery and style, but it was the man behind that leather jacket who made her heart pound ferociously. A boy from simple beginnings, who'd worked tirelessly to provide his mother an easier life. Without him, Morgan might never have confronted her inhibitions. Tears welled and her disappointment built. She didn't know how to face him, truly end it and say goodbye.

When she turned to leave, he glanced over. Chase couldn't mistake those curves. And he dashed after her, toward the Staples Center as an L.A. Kings game let out. She paced onto a crowded railway platform as a westbound train pulled in. As he followed, an outstretched arm intervened.

"Your card?" the weary-eyed transit officer asked.

"Morgan!" Chase shouted at her back as the train doors slid open. He scoured his wallet, recovered a transit pass and jammed it to the validator, but it failed to load. Jetting to a ticket machine, he frantically cut the line, much to the outrage of those waiting. Scrambling to add a fare, he looked back nervously, grateful as the train waited for a mass of passengers to board. Morgan wasn't visible, but with his pass properly loaded, he leaped through the nearest doorway, just making the doors.

As it started to move, Chase paced through several cars and spotted Morgan sandwiched between two massive, irate hockey fans. Encountering his eyes, she stood and stalked away. He pursued.

When he seized her shoulder, she whipped around and snarled, "Shouldn't you be off screwing your ex?"

"Do you seriously think I'd touch her?" he inquired, loud enough to garner attention. Things certainly looked bad with Tori at Lit Empire, but he hoped Morgan would hear him out. Meanwhile, several college students lifted phones to capture this celebrity sighting.

"I don't know who you'll hump if the price is right," she blurted, scowling. After a camera phone flashed, she pushed ahead. Again, he followed. She lowered her voice. "You're a jerk and a liar."

"Liar?" he asked.

When the train jolted to stop and some passengers stepped off, Morgan settled into a vacant seat.

"What lies?"

"The hold."

He stiffened. Just then, at a University of Southern California station, his coed fangirls stood. "Bye, Chase," one cooed with a juvenile wave before exiting.

Ignoring her, he sat beside Morgan. "I meant to mention the production hold."

Her sharp brown eyes could split a diamond. If looks could slay, he'd be road kill. "You realize I could have HIV?"

"I wanted to tell you! But since most holds are false positive tests, as in this instance, I didn't want to freak you out.

Not when Mandi had just invited me to meet your family."

She tilted her head. "I can appreciate that."

"It was selfish," he continued. "And I'm ashamed. But I knew how close you all were and I wanted to be part of that. I never had an enormous, affectionate family, with siblings and grandparents and cousins and cousin's cousins."

"The family isn't so loving right now," Morgan explained. "Not since stumbling upon Harrison Krol's true identity."

"So?"

"They're disgusted. My father isn't speaking to me."

Chase sighed. Erotica wasn't simply his bread and butter. Like a mayor becoming the face of a city or a news anchor representing the network, Chase Prince embodied porn. The Prince of Sin had replaced Harrison Krol more than a decade prior. He placed a hand on her leg. "Will you always be ashamed of my job?"

Morgan admired the distant, flickering Hollywood Hills. "I'm not ashamed. I was proud of you on set. But I also want to respect my parents."

He snorted. "You act liberal and progressive, but apparently it's all an act. Stop playing *woe is me*," he jabbed, raising both hands. "You're the one who identified Kali to spite me."

"What?"

"We all saw your feature."

Morgan had been avoiding technology to evade Chase and completely forgot about her feature. "I never mentioned Kali's name."

"Okay," he ridiculed. "So how did she get namedropped as a pathetic porn girl?"

Suddenly the train's stop and go had Morgan ready to puke. She placed herself at her desk, rushing to submit the feature after karaoke, after learning about the porn hold. Though admittedly distracted, Morgan couldn't believe she'd be so absent-minded as to accidentally type Kali's name in the script.

"You got your story wrong," he said. "Kali's nothing like that anymore."

Morgan flushed uncomfortably, forlorn for Kali. "I know she isn't, and I didn't use her name . . . If somehow it happened, it was accidental."

"OK, Ms. journalistic prowess." He pouted his contempt. "I'd love to believe the vlogger desperate for a promotion. You should have attacked me, not my friend."

"OK, I will attack you! There's plenty I can't stand about you."

"Lay it on me, darling," he dared, with a nostril flare and *bring it* hand wave.

She reminded herself that despite everything wonderful he'd done, despite a smoldering lower lip and those capable hands, he had lied about the porn hold and working with his ex. "Tori called me a *whore*!" Morgan spurted without falter. Perhaps she'd finally overcome that word.

The two elderly ladies knitting beside them gasped. Morgan sensed countless curious eyes but had nowhere to run. "You obviously told her about my past."

"I would never," he defended.

"Well, she was dangling that word around."

"For Tori, it's like any other word. And I wouldn't have touched her! When you showed up, I was making calls and got the shoot cancelled."

"What if it hadn't been cancelled? I already loathe the thought of you screwing other women." Her hands clawed at the air. "And worry it might one day be her."

He clasped her hands. "You keep circling back to my job."

"Well, it's a unique line of work." She freed her hands to tug those bangle bracelets. "Do you think I appreciate when you can't finish with me because you're working later?"

Chase exhaled. All his exes understood the trade. Porn

people socialized within their tribe because insiders grasped the unconventional stipulations. In many ways, dating industry women was simpler, although he'd never experienced emotions so consuming, deep or raw with a porn girl. "Morg, I thought we got past my career obstacles."

"You don't even like your job! Why do you think I bought you cinematography classes?"

"To convince me to quit performing?" he snapped, feeling manipulated. Wincing, he decided Sandra was right, Morgan might be a tad too bright.

"Not quit, but—"

"You're trying to change me," he spat.

"No, I believe in you."

"You're one to talk! You hate vlogging, yet are continuously sucked back in."

She mustered a slow nod. As the train pulled into polished downtown Santa Monica, she stood. "I think we rushed into this."

"Maybe," he said softly.

Their eyes met until she side-eyed him and huffed. He clenched his fists, tempted to restrain her against the window, almost considering one final tryst. But it seemed doubtful they could kiss and make up—or fornicate and make up.

"Farewell, dingus," she mumbled with a half-smirk before exiting the train.

Fireworks erupted at Santa Monica Pier, but Chase's eyes remained fixed on her until the doors clicked shut. He headed back downtown to retrieve his motorcycle.

Drained from what had already been an impossibly long night, they both rung in the new year separately and alone. Drowning in heartbreak, they were too proud to admit that maybe they'd made a mistake and accepted their happily never after . . .

CHAPTER NINETEEN: AFTER THE FALL

"They don't call it retail therapy for nothing!" Kaya gushed, handing the cashier a credit card. Morgan managed a weak smile and thanked Kaya for the new silk blouse and leather handbag necklace. After adding to a heap of shopping bags collected along New York City's Fifth Avenue, they zipped heavy down coats and exited the store. Through the January frost, they returned to their five-star Park-facing hotel. Accustomed to shopping trips with Mandi, Kaya delightedly indulged in her choice restoration remedy with her eldest daughter, who'd been miserable as of late.

Since New Year's, Morgan had hardly vacated her apartment. She'd spent a week replaying every moment, envisioning each detail, wondering *maybe, what if...* But between porn holds and randy reunions with exes, plus Al's disappointment, she couldn't envision a feasible *maybe* or *what if* for her and Chase.

Where Morgan's head understood, her heart disapproved. Emotional pain had never ached so physically, as though someone had reached into her exposed chest to wring every last droplet of blood from her passionate heart. Suddenly understanding lovesick clichés, Morgan had embraced them. She'd passed time devouring tubs of ice cream, watching angry chick flicks and rocking out to revenge-seeking country. After a failed attempt at cutting her own hair, Morgan had visited her stylist, who overhauled the ratty disaster into a chic bob. Adding to her disappointment, the few times she'd ventured into work, Jason avoided any promotion talk, despite her exposé's success. By week's end, Kaya had intervened with empty luggage and two plane tickets to JFK.

Morgan and Kaya returned to the hotel with dented bank accounts and higher spirits. After checking their bags, they hurried eagerly to afternoon tea. Reclined comfortably in traditional side chairs, they admired the airy indoor garden and vast windows that admitted brilliant natural light. The proper dignified sort surrounded them—wealthy tourists and Manhattan elite, primarily gray-haired women in expensive chapeaus who appeared fresh off a post-Edwardian film set.

Kaya chitchatted by flattering Morgan's new hairstyle, comparing New York to California and discussing some happenings back home. Morgan shuddered at the mention of Mandi, who'd returned to texting incessantly about revisiting Grant as a prospect. She'd eventually blocked Mandi's number.

Clearly, Kaya recognized Morgan's reaction. "Never mind your sister. Your foolish father, too. They will come around."

A server placed down a tiered mini sandwich platter and Morgan's brows rose in appreciation.

As Kaya's pale pink manicured nails picked apart a deviled egg sandwich, she changed the subject by humbly confessing, "I've known you were exploring the porn industry for well over a month now. I just didn't tell anybody."

"Seriously?" Morgan assumed Kaya told Al everything.

"Sweetie, I follow *Slander* regularly because of you. You think I couldn't figure out who Barbie Blue was?" Steeping an organic tea, Kaya beamed.

Morgan nodded, shocked and impressed by her mother's believable front.

"I've known *Harrison*'s identity quite a while now, as well."

"Since when?"

Kaya's lips pursed. "Since a day or two after meeting him."

"How?"

Prince of Sin

"You think your dear old mother has never viewed pornography?"

Morgan gagged on her pintsized sandwich and somehow resisted regurgitating it.

"There was a scene with several men," Kaya explained.

Horrified, Morgan froze.

"And this one helpless girl. It was a ludicrous plotline, some men using her as bait to lure the boyfriend who owed them money. Then I recognized Harrison, well, Chase, and I immediately exited the window."

Her mother had watched her naked ex-boyfriend laying pipe. Morgan couldn't move.

"I didn't much care for that scene anyhow. Locating pornography I enjoy is rather difficult," Kaya continued.

Processing her mom's naughty confession was rather difficult.

"For the most part it's extremely brutal and vile. It's challenging to find porn I relate to. I prefer more sensitive work."

Morgan never dreamed her prudish mother enjoyed an erotic side. "You have to know where to look, I guess," Morgan advised, though she wasn't sure how much relatable porn existed. Morgan's hand met her forehead. She was encouraging smut talk with mother dearest.

"I'll keep looking, then." Kaya squeezed a hand over Morgan's. "I feel extremely grateful to have you to discuss this sort of thing. I've never felt comfortable discussing it with anyone. Not even your father."

"Why not?" Morgan figured that's what partners were for, instead of daughters.

"Oh, we maintain our routine," Kaya said, giggling.

Face hidden behind a mug, Morgan cringed.

"I'm tremendously pleased with him. Our pattern does the trick. But work was your father's heartfelt passion. And mine was you girls. Growing older, I've explored my sexuality

159

elsewhere. It started with erotic romance films, like *Secretary* and *9 ½ Weeks* and evolved to pornography."

Gurgling her tea, Morgan realized the *Secretary* tape never belonged to Rosa. As Kaya pressed for more details from the porn world, Morgan sympathized for her mother, who couldn't discuss sex with her partner of nearly thirty years.

"Harrison? Baby?" Sandra Krol called out, entering Chase's cluttered apartment, which held spilled drinks and trash strewn. She hadn't heard from her son in three days, and so had come looking for him. In Chase's bedroom, she found him passed out, tangled in bed sheets. "Harrison?" Fiercely she shook his shoulders.

Since splitting from Morgan, Chase had hardly slept. Mostly, he'd been working. Dissociating from Lit Empire Entertainment had only made the Prince of Sin more desirable. With every studio in town pawing for Viola Emperor's not-so-sloppy seconds, he'd porked for pay daily. Work had distracted him from the dagger in his heart that kept twisting for kicks.

Between shoots, he'd worked out. But when he wasn't taking care of business or exercising, he'd sought distractions. Cocaine binges had followed. Occasionally he'd catch a few z's, but even in slumberland, he couldn't avoid Morgan's freckled nose or vehement encouragement.

He sat on a speeding railway train in a cartoonish universe. It screeched to a sparking halt at the base of a steep hill that rose beyond the clouds. Passengers soared through cars. Chase hopped off and pushed the caboose. Though he huffed and puffed, it remained unmoved.

Then Morgan appeared, sitting on a train car. "You got this," she said. "I believe in you." And so he exerted every ounce of energy he could muster until the train squeaked and lurched forward. With his greatest champion's words of support, he forced it uphill.

Chase stirred in bed.

"Harrison! Baby!" Sandra shouted.

He jolted awake in Sandra's guest bedroom, dripping in sweat. "How'd I get here?"

"You were in a stupor. I escorted you to my car and drove you," Sandra explained. "Are you doped up?"

"What time is it?" Opening his phone calendar, he breathed a relieved sigh at not having missed any shoots.

"Are you high, Harrison?" Sandra glared sternly, those gray locks held in a loose ponytail. She approved of marijuana or hashish but nothing harder.

"Just trying some all-natural performance enhancers," he lied.

Smacking him, she said, "You are taking dope, you dope."

Busted, he simply hung his head.

She frowned. "Feeling hungry?"

Comfortably seated at Sandra's kitchen table twenty minutes later, Chase devoured a bowl of Mac and Cheese, a childhood favorite. With her demanding work schedule, Sandra had rarely found time to cook, so familiar, easy macaroni became a longtime staple.

Nostalgic moments like this subtly reminded Chase why he chose a so-called *life of sin*. "There's cash for you at my place," he mumbled through a creamy, cheesy mouthful.

"Cash?" Sandra asked, rinsing a pot. "Baby, I earn sufficient income off my investments now. I don't need your money."

"Oh. That's great, then." He'd done more than enough to provide Sandra a comfortable life, but instead of ecstatic or relieved, his heart sank, severed. "Guess you don't need me anymore." When she kissed his forehead, it was clear that wasn't true.

Seated on the back-porch that evening, they admired a pink sunset. Light glinted off neighboring rooftops. Chase inhaled a distant, salty ocean breeze. How lucky they were. He regretted returning to drugs after several sober months. "Time for me to go."

"Where to?" Sandra asked, standing to hug her only baby.

"I have my first cinematography class tonight."

She beamed as they embraced.

As Morgan researched potential travel destinations on a summerlike mid-January afternoon, someone pounded unexpectedly at her apartment door. Through the peephole she spotted Grant.

"Hi there," she said, opening up.

"Helloooo," Grant bellowed, stepping inside.

"Care for a drink?" she offered politely, directing him to the couch. She faulted Kaya and Al for raising her with proper manners when she wanted to ask him to leave.

"No, thank you." He settled down. "I was in your neighborhood."

"You happened to be in this neighborhood?" she asked, brow raised.

"To meet with several Silicon Beach companies, yes. And after learning you'd been down lately, I wanted to do something nice."

"Learning from Mandi?" She resented her sister's not-so-subtlety.

"From your incredible mother, actually. We were introduced at the club."

With Kaya behind the surprise drop-in, his gesture morphed from irritating to kind. Though Morgan wondered what *do something nice* entailed.

Half an hour later, they boarded a thirty-six-foot cruising sailboat in Marina del Rey, an affluent harbor-side community, home to thousands of small craft vessels. Older couples canoodled on ocean-view balconies as dog walkers paced pathways that hugged the marina and sightseers sipped cocktails on chic bistro patios.

As Grant donned a fancy sailor's hat, Morgan admired his nautical style of a striped tee, white trousers and gold-buttoned navy blazer. Leaving the harbor, they enjoyed a gorgeous, sunny winter day.

Ever chatty, Grant recounted his prior meetings with three innovative startups. He wanted to invest in something unique and wasn't sure these companies had edge. Enthralled by his passion, Morgan listened attentively, talking him through each potential investment's pros and cons.

The air grew chillier and Grant draped an arm over her. "Thank you for bringing me out today," she said. "I'm having a wonderful time. But I'm not ready to date." Surrounded by the vast ocean, she felt comfortable admitting her sorrow aloud. Caged in her apartment, she'd been hiding.

Grant swiftly sidled away, placing both hands in his lap. "I appreciate your honesty," he said. "I'm having a wonderful time, as well. The opinion of someone who broke free from Orange County is refreshing. Your input is of great value, Morgan. Could we please remain friends?"

He extended a professional hand. She enjoyed Grant's company and hoped if they shook, he'd indeed keep things platonic. Clutching his hand, she maintained, "Friends."

"Next week we'll discuss Westerns," Professor Rosenthal announced. "Everybody please watch *High Noon* and *The Searchers* and read these articles." As his classmates stood, Chase followed, grabbing a handout off the teacher's desk before exiting.

Almost skipping toward the parking garage, he embraced this change of pace. With a rich past, Romanesque architecture, shady trees and enthusiastic pupils, the campus radiated a more promising vibe than other L.A. locales he frequented.

Reading the course syllabus left him giddy, eager to complete his initial assignment. He never knew learning could be so inspiring. His sharpest middle school memories were classes so boring he'd ditch to make out with high school cheerleaders at a nearby park. By high school, he'd graduated to teachers and backseats of cars.

Naturally, Chase wanted to tell Morgan about such an inspiring first class. As an alternative, he sped downtown to see his mentor.

In his dark office, Jimmy huddled behind a computer screen like a deer in headlights. Bulging, bloodshot eyes proved he hadn't moved in hours. "How long you been caged in this lair?" Chase asked, walking in.

"Huh?" Jimmy responded, eyes fixed on pixels. "Oh. Hey, mate."

"Where's the Meatball?"

Jimmy glanced up. "Bob? The meatball to my . . . spaghetti?"

"Bingo." Chase tapped his nose one time. "And Kali's the parmesan cheese you *wish* you could sprinkle all over that entree."

After a chuckle, Jimmy explained, "Bob left hours ago."

"Have you been here all night?"

"Not like I have a bird to scuttle home to." Jimmy stood to pour two cups of tea.

"I just had my first cinematography class!" Chase touted excitedly.

Jimmy grinned proudly. "Good on ya! Next thing I know, I'll be competing with you for gigs."

Rubbing his neck, Chase stared at his shoes. "I don't know about that." His stature shrank, a mere neophyte next to

Jimmy's real deal. "My professor said I need a video camera and editing software. Do you think I could borrow your equipment occasionally?"

"Of course!" Jimmy insisted, handing over a mug. "You can always find me here."

Chase frowned. "No new women to take dancing?" he asked hopefully, though Jimmy never dated seriously. "Or whatever it is old fart Brits do to court ladies."

"We can't all be studs like you." Jimmy returned to his desk. "A Joe Schmo smut director like me, well, industry gals only shag me to score gigs. And civilians, once I tell them what I do, they run for the Hollywood Hills." Jimmy continued editing. "For most of us smut blokes, it's a solitary existence."

As Chase watched Jimmy laser-focus on an erotic video that would likely get lost someplace on the worldwide web, he stung for his hardworking mentor's isolation.

Chapter Twenty: Royal Reunion?

K ali entered a plain Santa Monica office building and stepped into a quiet entryway. She scanned a directory index board, where *Slander* was not listed.

That was when Morgan emerged.

"You set me up, civilian?"

"Would you have spoken to me otherwise?" Morgan had had Sean call Kali, pretending *Slander* had some fan mail from the feature. He'd sent her a false address to retrieve it.

"I knew this sounded shady." Kali turned to leave.

"Wait!" Morgan grabbed her shoulder. "Don't leave."

Kali whipped around. "Why, civilian? You are using me to get to Chase?"

"Let's keep him out of it." Constructing this plan, Morgan had vowed not to ask about him, no matter how challenging.

"Then why I should stay? So you can make up more lies?"

"I never lied," Morgan explained. "My story submission never cited you. How you got namedropped, I'm not sure. But I am investigating the matter." She assumed Marcus was involved but required proof.

Sizing her up, Kali bitterly said, "Fine, thank you. That is all?" Half-waving, she turned to exit.

"Actually, there's one more thing."

Morgan stepped upstairs and Kali followed, intrigued.

"This is how I got my *legs*," Morgan explained, opening the door to her pole studio. A scantily clad teacher and several students, fit and flexible women of various shapes and sizes, stretched on yoga mats.

"Why you bring me here?" asked Kali.

"I registered you for a pole class." Smiling hopefully, Morgan rendered a cloth bag with workout apparel, hoping Kali's curiosity would prevail. "Do it just for you," she added with a now flawless wink. Kali's face remained tight, but she grabbed the bag and raced into a change room.

Ten minutes later, Kali shimmied and stretched, warming up in black spandex shorts and a sports bra. Afterward, Morgan demonstrated a few introductory moves. Kali was certainly a beginner, sexercise being her only form of cardio in half a decade. She landed turns awkwardly and off kilter but was strong and motivated, always trying again.

"Guess I was wrong," Morgan admitted. "I doubted you'd be into this."

"You got a lot wrong, civilian."

Morgan sighed.

"Using my name in that story did not anger me," Kali explained. "*How* you used it disappointed me. You make me seem like some tragic, troubled girl, needing for attention. That is how you see me?"

"Not at all," Morgan said.

"I love wild, kinky sex." Kali smirked lustfully. Anyone who'd seen Kali's pep talk and performance during the gangbang shoot would know she'd been more engaged in that scene than anyone else. "Doing porn, I get to explore my fantasies. Does society approve or my family love it? Fuck no! But I am not some lost porn girl. My work is my love and I wish your story detailed that passion." Kali attempted another spin and, landing smoothly, cheered, "Yes!"

"It's impressive, and honorable, that you perform to take control and satisfy your own needs. Many people suppress their carnal desires." After discovering her mother's sexual shackles, Morgan knew the blessing of exploring her fantasies with Chase. "I wish I'd explored the whole story of women in porn, not just the grim side. I'm so sorry," Morgan said genuinely. "Thank you for explaining."

Kali examined her eyes.

"Maybe I could write a new piece, clear things up and—"

"Not needed," Kali said. "Thank you, legs. Now, teach me to climb this stupido thing."

Morgan beamed, grateful to be *legs* again. She demonstrated a basic climb. Kali attempted it with drive and ambition. Beyond Kali's tact, Morgan respected her for daring to pursue controversial dreams.

Growing increasingly lethargic at work, Morgan compiled a list of *Ten Hollywood Hot Spots to Spot a Celeb*. Surprisingly, she missed the smut circus. Swiveling in her desk chair, she surveyed the office and recounted years of memories, like when some YouTube star's peeved manager barged in and slammed a door, shattering a wall clock. She stared at the clock's former post. Two years later, it still hadn't been replaced. Once bustling and exciting, *Slander*'s office felt more like a dungeon now.

As Morgan considered a potential tenth hot spot, she recalled where one might spot celeb Chase Prince—Venice Beach, Grieta Profunda Canyon, Jimmy's studio, *Slander*, a women's shelter, his mother's house, *her* mother's house. She smirked recalling her spectacular ass-plop after sighting him at the holiday party. He'd astonished her that night, casually winning everyone over.

"In here, Sidney!" Jason shouted. With a side-eye, she trudged toward his office. Scarcely glancing from a newspaper, he stated, "We need someone at Pornopalooza."

After her exposé, Morgan had presumed he'd send another body to the annual Pornopalooza conference. Considering Jason, she should have known better.

"Your room is already booked," he said.

"My room?" Morgan crossed her arms.

"Yes. It starts tomorrow in Vegas. Your flight leaves in the morning."

"Am I going as a *producer*?" she asked, tired of dancing around it.

Jason's eyes finally darted up. "I'll compile the paperwork while you're gone." She tilted her head skeptically. "Expect a new contract on your desk when you return." Brows lifted, he anticipated her delight.

"Good," she responded, blinking rapidly to mask jittery excitement. "And moving forward, I'll need final approval before anything goes live. No names or details added without my consent, like this Kali fiasco." Jason had promised to investigate exactly how Kali's name crept into her feature but came up empty. She still assumed Marcus's involvement.

"Of course," Jason said, returning to the newspaper. "That must not happen again."

Scurrying home to pack, Morgan shivered with both dread and titillation at a prospective reunion with Mr. Prince of Sin, in Sin City itself.

"Final boarding call to Las Vegas," a flight attendant droned over crackly speakers.

Chase missed the announcement, too engrossed in a scene from *Fargo* on his iPad, noting various shots for an extra credit assignment. Countless so-so porn directors produced mediocre, unremarkable products. They were stones in a quarry. The rare greats were precious gems. Chase had worked for both and knew which he wanted to be.

"Last call for Vegas!" the attendant beckoned, glaring.

Stepping onboard, Chase spotted familiar faces — girls he'd banged and dudes he'd crossed swords with. Passing Martini McPie and Tiger Trece, he wondered if they had met. He knew Martini would love Tiger's superstar status and Tiger would appreciate her fresh-faced innocence. They'd shoot a magnificent scene together, he realized.

Taking his seat, Chase opened a notebook and jotted their names. Glancing around, he recognized more faces. He wondered if Mark Harder had ever worked with Lindsey Velour. Mark had entered the industry right around Lindsey's recent maternity absence. With a similar love for anal, Chase reckoned they'd perform flawlessly together. And so, like a hockey coach determining the lineups before a game, Chase used first-hand industry knowledge to match pairs and groups that would have outstanding chemistry in his future films.

After packing, Morgan beat the afternoon rush down to Orange County. This time, she vowed to be honest about her assignment. When she arrived at Al and Kaya's house, a shower was running upstairs, so she waited in the living room.

Al's clippings notebooks sat on the coffee table. All the stories he'd ever written were taped inside. Morgan flipped through several. There were interviews with mayors and senators, policy change editorials, O.J. trial coverage and sports stories covering California teams, local and professional. She knew about Al's impressive, fulfilling career, but each article sequentially laid out was awe-inspiring.

Al came downstairs in a housecoat. "That was one tough interview," Al stated, referring to a one-on-one with a convicted killer. "He'd just been sentenced to death."

Morgan skipped several pages. "Another toughie," he revealed, donning reading glasses and settling beside her. It was coverage of the Rodney King riots. "Such a horrendous, tragic week."

He opened another book and turned to coverage of the Anaheim Ducks 2007 Stanley Cup win. "In more than thirty-five years, this was one of my favorites."

When he smiled, his forehead skin and dark brown eyes crinkled — wrinkles that had been hard-earned.

"Mine too," she said. They'd attended Game Five together and witnessed the franchise's first Stanley Cup win.

As they continued through each book, Al recounted newsroom ethics debates won or lost and tales of ridiculous interviewees. His obvious passion radiated with each tale. When he closed the last book, Morgan blurted, "You'll be pleased to know Chase and I broke up."

He glanced curiously. "I'm only pleased if you are."

"I thought you didn't approve?"

"It's your outrageous lies that I don't approve of," he said. "But whom you date is your choice. If you believe in your work and relationship, and are honest about them, I stand behind you one hundred percent."

Morgan leaned on his shoulder.

"There is nothing respectable about deceit," he continued. "If you can't stand behind your choices, why should anybody else?"

She nodded and responded, "Moving forward, I'll always be straight with you." As Al rubbed her arm, she told him about Las Vegas.

On the drive home, she stopped for gas. While paying inside the shop, a cheap rag mag cover caught her eye. In the corner, a tiny photo showed Tori Jade kissing Chase Prince's cheek over the caption *Royal Reunion?*. Tempted to purchase it, she knew reading about them would only quash her ever-slowly mending heart. Tears pooled. It was time to accept that Chase had moved on while she struggled without him.

Returning to the car, Morgan recalled that afternoon at sea with Grant. She pressed the phone button. "Call Grant Wexler."

Chapter Twenty-One: Porno-palooza

Hosted by a different city each year, the epic Pornopalooza conference was all business for trade vendors. But it was also an opportunity for devoted fans to meet their favorite stars or explore taboo desires.

After checking into a hotel, Grant and Morgan ventured to the conference's bustling main hall. No sooner had they entered than a cougar wearing dildo necklaces approached to unbutton Grant's tailor-fit dress shirt. Morgan laughed as he guided the determined lady aside.

With endless booths and scheduled seminars, it could have been any trade show, if not for giant penis paraphernalia and women flashing any camera that passed. And then some.

As Morgan and Grant explored together, each booth vied for their attention, from breast lift stickers to discreet teddy bear toys. Grant stopped to discuss investment opportunities with an erotic chocolate vendor, so Morgan strolled ahead. Spotting the *Benny's Babes* platform, she strode over.

"Legs!" Kali said before they exchanged cheek kisses.

"Kali," a calm passerby said, approaching. In her mid-forties, the woman sported short dark hair, olive skin, thick eyebrows and an expansive, affectionate smile.

"Aria!" Kali belted. They kissed gently on the lips, lingering longer than a polite peck. Finally, Kali introduced Morgan, blabbered something in Italian, then sauntered away to flirt with some stiff, gray-haired suits.

"What do you do?" Morgan inquired.

"I am a feminist pornographer," Aria stated.

"What's that?" Morgan asked. "Can those two words even be uttered together?"

"Come." Aria led her to the nearby *Fetching Films* booth. "This is my company. We produce feminist porn."

Expecting tame, slow lovemaking, Morgan found nothing soft about it. On one screen, an impassioned man tugged a woman's ponytail while fucking her roughly from behind. Morgan edged back.

"You've never seen feminist or couple's porn?" Aria asked.

"No. And I expected it to be soft kisses."

"Feminist porn emphasizes women as equals. Both on camera and on set. That doesn't mean it can't be rough or raunchy."

The performance mesmerized Morgan, who watched intently as cameras closed in on both partners' delighted faces. There were no innocent girls getting taken advantage of at fake auditions or in dark alleyways. It was aggressive but beautiful and highlighted both partners' climaxes.

"You created this?"

Nodding, Aria asked, "Are you a feminist?"

"I guess," Morgan responded weakly.

"You don't sound so sure."

Morgan considered her uncertainty and explained, "As a progressive young professional woman, I know I'm *supposed* to be a feminist. But part of me associates feminism with unrelatable bra-burning hippies."

"Do you think men and women should have equal rights?"

"Undoubtedly," Morgan responded.

"Then you are a feminist. Simple as that." Aria waved her hands. "People are terrified of that word, of radical feminist agendas. But it's not about being better than men or hating them. It's about equity. It means appreciating issues *both* genders face."

Aria picked up several DVDs and Morgan admired the covers, which were anything but tame. One revealed a collared woman on a leash. Another featured a naked couple's shadows by a fire. Eager to gift the DVDs to Kaya, Morgan placed them in her bag.

"We need more hardworking women to support our movement, if you are interested."

"How do you know I'm hardworking?" Morgan asked.

Aria huffed. "Kali doesn't associate with ordinary women."

Morgan's thoughts spun like a mouse on a wheel. She considered joining the feminist porn movement by creating erotica for women too ashamed to admit to watching porn or who struggled to find enjoyable material. Women like herself, or Kaya. And she had ideas for reaching a female audience, like free trial subscriptions or live-blogging shoots or running social campaigns for women to submit scene ideas. "I have a million thoughts," Morgan explained.

"You should read this," Aria said firmly, revealing a feminist porn book. "Learn what the women who started the movement achieved. It will help you get started, if that's true interest I see in your eyes."

"Oh, it is." Mind abuzz, Morgan thanked Aria and scurried off to start reading. She weighed helping feminist pornographers like Aria market their work against producing her own original material. To create fresh feminist porn, she would need financial assistance. Plus a director. Morgan knew exactly who longed to direct this type of porn, *real couples, having real sex*. High from the excitement, she contemplated asking him.

Chase grew jaded at the Prince of Sin booth, where eager reporters asked repetitive questions, shrewd businessmen pitched tacky joint ventures and fangirls snapped selfies. After discussing a favorable opportunity down under with an Australian pornographer, Chase headed to the food court for a much-needed break. As he approached a pretzel stand, sparkly, pungent, tiara-clad Tori blocked him. He attempted a swerve, but she wouldn't allow it.

"Did you read our piece in *V.I.P.*?" she asked.

He massaged his neck and gazed forward, eager to escape. "What?"

"Our tabloid story, silly. That says we're back together." Leaning in, she giggled and whispered, "I was the anonymous tipster."

"Get over me already."

"Is that what you're commanding of all your exes?"

His arms instantly flailed. "What are you talking about?"

She pointed triumphantly to Morgan and Grant sharing a snack. Chase frowned, instantly recognizing *Kiss Cam* dude. His hunger pains stirred into throbbing heartache and jealousy. Since breaking up, Chase had strived to forget Morgan's side-eye glares, sass, that single upper lip freckle . . . But he couldn't escape her drive and passion, because it continued to shape him. How the broken-hearted heartbreaker longed to discuss his film class with her. Or march over, punch *Kiss Cam* bro's face and kiss her wildly.

"Can we play now?" Tori whined, seizing his hand.

"What about Viola? Or should I say, your beloved, protective Master?"

"I dumped that saggy ass, ratchet biatch," Tori squeaked. "She was *so* controlling, plus like a hundred years old." She strategically placed his finger between her teeth.

Chase watched Morgan sporting a smart new hairstyle and conversing emphatically with Grant. Yearning to escape heartbreak and craving anything to improve his spirits, he allowed sprightly Tori Jade to steer him toward an elevator.

As Morgan raved to Grant about Aria and feminist porn, she inadvertently caught Tori and Chase's exit and thus figured the tabloid rumor must be accurate. And so, she decided not to approach Chase about her thrilling plans. Luckily, Grant was providing useful tips for starting a successful business.

Just then, Sean video called her. She excused herself to better hear him. Rushing down a hallway, she passed Kali's enthusiastic Q&A with fans and reporters before stepping outside to find a quiet place to sit.

"O-M-G, sweetums!" Sean exclaimed. "How's 'palooza?"

"Going great!"

"Good, because I have some abysmal *Slander* tea."

So intoxicated by feminist porn, Morgan had forgotten about her actual job.

"Jason let it slip that *he* rummaged through your notes and *he* slid Kali's name in your feature. Marcus had nothing to do with it."

Her livid eyes widened. "Could you put Jason on?"

"You denounce him, girl!" Sean responded with a spirited snap.

Just yards away, Kali proudly lived her truth, as Al had done throughout his career. Morgan needed to do the same. No longer could she allow a conniving boss to string her along, betray her contacts' trust and deceive her out of promised promotions. Finally, she was done acquiescing and living *Slander*'s seedy truth.

Jason's haughty face emerged onscreen with Sean peering over his shoulder. "How's my favorite vlogger?" he asked indifferently, reading something on his phone.

She cringed, denouncing that title forever. "I'm fantastic, because I quit."

Awestruck, Jason looked up. "You are quitting on me?"

Behind him, Sean fist pumped encouragingly and mouthed, *Yas, Queen!*

"I know it doesn't sound like something I'd say, but I'm done."

"What?!" he growled.

Morgan waved facetiously, disconnected and stared at the cellphone in her shaky palm. Her neck softened as though a hundred pounds just lifted off it. She wished she'd quit ages prior but at least had finally done it. Grinning, she scurried inside, eager to celebrate.

Princess Tori Jade slurped pure happy powder through a hundred-dollar bill and up a dehydrated nostril, where it penetrated her bloodstream to stimulate that narcissistic brain. Splayed naked in a hot tub, aside from her tiara, she lined more cocaine along the marble ledge.

Seated out of the water, Chase observed. Behind him, open glass doors revealed a deluxe rock star suite, elaborately decorated with cutting-edge furniture and accessories. Outside vast windows, the Vegas Strip shimmered below.

"Have some," Tori insisted.

But the neatly aligned, chalky white crumbs repulsed him. Just months ago, he would have inhaled every granule, then pounded Tori and any girlfriends she invited along. But he no longer felt inclined. Now, this airbrushed cokehead sloshing about seemed pathetic and desperate for attention.

"Get in here," she purred with a come-hither finger. "Stop pouting with those green eyes."

"I only have one green eye," Chase corrected.

"So?" She looked dully through him, swished over and unzipped his fly. "This is the only muscle I give a fuck about."

But he jumped away. "Well I have no more fucks left to give you."

"What?" she barked.

"We're different people, Tor," he tried to politely explain. "I have to go."

"You are not abandoning me!" She stood defiantly. Sharp fingernails met her forehead and she clawed down her own face, leaving a bloody trail. "Walk out that door and I tell security you did this."

Chase shook his head at her empty threat. Tori Jade would never risk any negative media attention. "Too bad only your pussy's insured, Princess," he said. Some hustler had once convinced Tori to purchase a costly vagina policy.

He hurried out, to locate the woman who truly knew him and his potential. Now, before he lost her forever.

Chapter Twenty-Two: Home Movies

Chase burst into Pornopalooza, where most booths had closed for the day. Jogging around, he peered eagerly down each abandoned aisle. A crowd watched a stage performance, so he sprinted over and spun people around, searching. Eventually, he slogged defeatedly to exit.

Passing the elevated stage, he looked up to Morgan, a contestant in some couple's challenge with Grant. Rushing up a side staircase, Chase hoped to pull her aside and grasped Morgan's shoulder from behind. As she turned in confusion, Grant swung and punched the Prince of Sin's face in front of several hundred awed spectators. As cameras flashed, Chase dropped to the floor.

He came to on a chair backstage.

"My apologies, bud. I was caught off guard," Grant said.

"What happened?" Chase asked, fidgety and anxious.

"I knocked you out cold, man."

Morgan appeared with an ice pack and pressed it to Chase's swollen purple and yellow chin. "Grant fights MMA, dingus," she explained.

With a perceptive nod, Grant stepped aside.

"Let's meet up tomorrow," she told him, sitting beside Chase as Grant exited.

Playful memories calmed Chase as he inhaled honey, vanilla aromas. "Tomorrow?" he asked. "You aren't sharing a room with that meathead?"

"Meathead? He's a brilliant investor, who I brought here to find new business opportunities. You thought I was with Grant?"

Chase's eyes shifted.

"Aren't you with Tori?"

"Reading *V.I.P.* were we?" he asked. "You of all people should know not to believe tabloid speculations."

She chuckled at the irony.

Chase lightly tugged a strand of her bob and noted, "You look so sophisticated." As he admired her smart, professional pant suit, his eyes found her cleavage. He didn't miss those baggy sweaters one bit.

Her eyes followed his gaze. "Let me take you to your room." She helped him stand.

Walking a foot apart, they crossed the hotel lobby silently, both masking glee at this reunion. Playfully, he nudged into her. With a smirk, Morgan kept pacing forward.

In the elevator, her gaze briefly shifted to the lower lip that had haunted her dreams for weeks. Then it found those brawny arms that once pressed her body against a mountain before savagely seizing it.

Finally, they reached his penthouse suite, where Chase held the door open. Her body fancied following him in, but her head knew better.

With a wink, he said, "I've missed you struggling to act professional around me, darling."

"Funny," she jabbed. "I haven't missed you or your arrogant winking."

"Then you shouldn't have a problem stepping inside."

He was blatantly playing her, but she willingly took the bait and entered. Majestic and sharp, this was easily the most badass hotel suite she'd ever seen. Plush white rugs covered dark hardwood floors. Distant dance music and a light breeze flowed in through open sliding glass doors that led to a vast, wraparound balcony. Between a pool table, hot tub and sauna, the amenities were abundant.

Chase sat on a gray leather sofa as Morgan wet a washcloth. She wiped the dry blood from his nose. When her finger grazed his lip, he licked it. Nervously, she tossed the washcloth to the floor.

"I started my film course," he revealed. "Oh, and Viola Emperor threatened my career, dropping me from Lit Empire. It backfired, though. I've never been more desired." Morgan listened intently, nodding enthusiastically. "But you know what I felt as Viola told me I'd never perform again?"

Morgan shrugged.

"Relief. And hope that I'd finally channel my energy into directing." Chase laughed breezily and boisterously with a carefree aura. He'd never discussed work with such a loose jaw and relaxed shoulders. Morgan beamed off his fervor.

He tugged her to sit beside him and explained, "Until you came along, I never thought that way."

As he leaned close, she breathed in minty freshness and lost herself in those hypnotic contrasting eyes. Their lips almost met, but neither dared make the first move. Once they relented, they'd be powerless.

Eventually she slid away and revealed, "I quit my job."

"When?"

"Like, an hour ago."

"Wow! Congrats, Morg. Finally. Are you happy?"

She jumped up and paced around. "Ecstatic! It came out of nowhere and it's such a thrill. I'm done! Do you know Kali's friend, Aria?"

He shook his head while admiring her wide, awakened eyes as she paced.

"Aria is amazing. She inspired me to create feminist porn."

"Seriously?"

"Yes!"

"Can I help?" he asked, feeding off her infectious enthusiasm. She looked the way he felt after his first cinematography class.

"Perhaps," she responded breathily.

Chase pulled her into his lap and instinctively slipped a hand above her behind. Spotting that lip freckle, he yearned to graze it tenderly. "Just perhaps?"

"Obviously you would make an astounding, talented business partner. But could we work together with that I.O.U. hanging over us?"

"I.O.U.?" he asked.

"Yes, if you recall that long overdue third fantasy?"

Morgan entered the bedroom through balcony doors in a red silk nighty and black fishnet stockings she'd purchased earlier that day. She sauntered to Chase, who sat on the bed holding a camcorder.

"Sure you want to do this?" he asked.

Putting a finger to his mouth, she responded, "Only if I keep the footage."

He raised his brows and started filming as she switched on a sexy R&B playlist. To the beat, she confidently slipped out of the soft slip to reveal a red pushup bra, matching thong and black lace garter belt. He whistled.

Taking the camera, she said, "Your turn. I'll direct."

He leaned casually on his forearms. "OK, director, what's my scene?"

"Your ex-girlfriend is considering taking you back," she explained, focusing the lens. "But only once she's been fully pleased."

"And what will please her?"

"Strip," she demanded. Her body ached as he lifted his t-shirt to reveal rock-hard abs. She noted they looked more cut than just weeks earlier. He tossed the shirt and smoothed his hair. "Don't," Morgan insisted. "I like you disheveled."

"My turn," he said, stealing the camera. "Get me out of these jeans." He lay on elegant throw pillows as she crawled forward. Staring into the lens, she licked her lips and unzipped his fly. "You're a natural," he encouraged.

Before Chase, Morgan had found playfulness in bed, especially with a camera, terrifying. But after weeks apart, there was no mistaking that he was her safe place. She tugged his jeans off and surprisingly found white boxer briefs. "No more black BBs?"

"I'm changing things up," he explained while she unclasped and dropped her bra.

Plucking the camera, she pointed it on him. "Kiss me here," she insisted, rubbing a finger around one hardening nipple, then the other. "And here."

He grabbed her waist and spun her onto the lavish cushions, then softly pecked each raspberry pink nipple. Her head fell back as she moaned saucily, movie star Morgan outshining Barbie Blue. Chase kissed from torso to thong as he leisurely unclasped both garter belts.

"Mmmm," she hummed wistfully. After weeks of excruciating withdrawal, she craved his fullness.

His fingers grazed her moistening lace panties. "Touch yourself," he ordered, pointing the camera at her slender curves. She obliged, slipping a hand under the soft fabric to slowly rub her clit. "Faster," he demanded. "Harder."

Morgan bit her lip, circled voraciously and tugged her wild mane of hair. He cherished this unravelling but soon felt excluded. "Let me help," he said, placing the camera down to retrieve a blue G-spot vibrator from a bedside table drawer.

"Finally using your scepter again?" she asked.

"I tossed it," he responded, slathering the toy with coconut oil. "This new toy matches the new me. Some woman I once worked with inspired the color." He winked. "Barbie Blue."

As he thumbed her budding clit, he switched the toy on. She shivered as the humming trinket entered her body. With deep breaths and curled toes, her entire body tightened. He knew exactly where to go.

"Not yet," he cautioned when she nearly climaxed. Removing the toy, he pulled his hands away and brought his face up to hers. Through a deep sigh, she whined despondently. Chase's soft lips delicately kissed hers, but she grabbed his head, latched onto his lower lip and sucked ferociously.

Relishing the intensity, he grinded his thick bulge against her clitoris, pressing the teasing lace fabric back and forth. Rapidly, she tugged his briefs down and he did away with her thong. He picked up the camcorder and flipped onto his back as her mouth went straight for that unmistakable cock. She sucked firm and fast. Before long, she pulled back to declare, "I need you inside me already."

Chase bared a condom and attempted to film her mouth coyly rolling it down his stiff shaft. Teeming with ecstasy, he slumped back. As Morgan slowly squatted down his length, he captured her euphoric, relieved smile. Starting gently, she worked up to a rapid pace.

After a minute, she climbed off to bend forward. "That the best you can do?" she patronized playfully, glancing back.

So he put the camera down and stood to penetrate from behind. Thrusting forcefully, he pressed her head into pillows and spanked that perky round ass. Soon she flipped over to take him in missionary, brimming on the edge while pulverizing her clit. Her round breasts jiggled and he took in the luscious sight. His imagination never did her figure justice.

Taking the camera, he recorded her frenzied face and body as his knob teasingly slipped in and out. Until finally a tight face and trembling body revealed her climax with one loud, boundless moan. Chase admired his roaring lioness, taking a moment to appreciate having Morgan back. "Wow," he said.

Breathily she demanded, "Finish in my mouth. And get it on tape."

Tilting his head in surprise, he continued to pump, nearing the brink. After pulling out, he rolled the condom off and filmed her lips meeting the tip. After a few quick sucks, he burst, eyes swirling back. He attempted recording it but distractedly rode waves of an epic climax.

Following a hot shower, Chase and Morgan cuddled in bed, devouring room service like they'd devoured each other. Playing back their sex tape, they laughed as Chase filmed the floor during the money shot.

"Five stars, two thumbs up," Morgan raved, mimicking a movie trailer voiceover. "The couple's chemistry is unmatched."

"Did he please the ex-girlfriend?" he asked, eyes pleading. "Does she take him back?"

"Maybe?"

"Why maybe?"

"Getting over you has been unimaginable," she admitted. "I'm barely there. I couldn't do it again."

"You won't have to. It won't end this time," he promised, squeezing her hands. "We're complete together. Let's be a team."

"But we have so many issues."

His heart lightened at the word *we*. He preferred when they were *we*. "Issues can't build up and then explode, like on the train."

She threw a hand to her forehead. "That was pretty humiliating."

"We'll have to work on that whole communication thing."

"And silly tabloid rumors need to be verified before we stupidly believe anything," she added self-deprecatingly.

They both chuckled.

"I'll never keep anything from you again," Chase insisted. "I'm sorry I ever did." When he winked and she scrunched her nose, Chase added, "Darling, you love my arrogant wink, admit it."

Returning a cheeky sidelong glance, she said, "You love my side-eye sass. Admit it, darling."

EPILOGUE

M organ had always enjoyed airports. Even mundane security screenings left her anticipating the next adventure. Travelling solo from Los Angeles to New York City six
months later, she was meeting Aria to help develop *Fetching
Films'* new marketing plan.

Across town in a small, rented Hollywood studio, Chase
Prince was directing his third porn scene, following the success of *Canyon Copulation* and *Playful Pole*. Today's shoot was
an erotic film within a film — a couple taping a home movie.

Everything had been a whirlwind since Morgan and the
Prince of Sin, or *Morgsin* (as Sean coined them), joined forces
at Pornopalooza to form Side-Eye Wink Productions. The
company's two generous investors, Grant Wexler and Al Sidney, had gotten the ball rolling. But Side-Eye Wink was thriv-
ing off Chase's artistic sensibility and Morgan's marketing
prowess. As the business had grown, voyeuristic non-porn
couples had started calling, asking for Side-Eye Wink to produce private sex tapes.

Before takeoff, Morgan texted Chase to ask about the shoot.
Going great. Safe flight, darling.

When her phone buzzed again, she looked down to a winking emoji and smiled.

The End

THIS BOOK WOULD NOT HAVE BEEN POSSIBLE WITHOUT THE FOLLOWING WEB SEARCHES:

other words for pubic hair
sexiest Greek Gods
words describing strong women
how do men dress
types of clothes hippies wear
porn director interview
other ways to say dumped
parts of a mountain/hill
eye shapes
nose bruise (images)
body part navel
where is the nape of the neck
slang for bitch
how do drugs leave your system
things to do instead of shake your head
ways to describe wet vaginas
patio furniture
punk rock fashion
best music for recording home sex video
where is the pelvis (images)
who was Cleopatra
what are butt implants made from
cloud 9 expression
restroom or washroom US

types of beards
what is a hip replacement
crazy hotel suites
do animals do gangbangs
things you feel in love
fingerbang
and many, many more.

You may also enjoy the following from eXtasy Books Inc:

A Melody for Adrian
Cherie Summers

Excerpt

"Your full name please."

"Melody Anne Stewart."

"Where did you attend school prior to River View?"

"I've been attending a boarding school for the last six years. Just outside of London, England."

Looking up from the enrollment form she'd been filling out, Mrs. Walters—one of River View's guidance counselors—pushed her bifocals back onto the bridge of her nose. "Did you say London?"

"Yes, ma'am." Beaming brightly, Melody pulled out a file folder from her notebook. "I brought my school records with me."

Folding her hands in her lap, she patiently watched Mrs. Walters scan her file.

"Why on earth would your parents send you to school so far away?"

"Why wouldn't they? The Chappell School for Girls has the finest reputation, and my father always believes in going with the best."

The counselor glanced back up at her and seemed to force a smile. "Why did your family now decide to send you to a public school? There are a number of fine private schools here in town."

"My sister graduated from here six years ago," Melody explained. "Leigh Stewart. Did you know her?"

Mrs. Walters shook her gray head. "Sorry, this is only my fourth year here."

"Well, it was her idea. She convinced my parents that I should spend at least one year of high school at home with my family. She also told them I needed to meet people from all walks of life, and public school seemed the best way to do that."

"Well, Melody, your sister seems wise. I hope you'll enjoy your last year here with us. But it will be quite different from what you're used to."

"I'm sure it will be." She lowered her gaze and stared at her shaking hands. It had been hard to say goodbye to all her friends.

Mrs. Walters must have sensed her apprehension. "The move was probably a little traumatic, and leaving the familiar behind will be difficult. If you ever need anyone to talk to, come see me. I'm here to help."

"Of course, thank you. I'll definitely need some advice about applying for colleges and taking the correct exams."

"Are you making plans for college?"

Melody's smile returned. "Oh yes, I've always wanted to go to medical school. Maybe become a pediatrician."

"Well, with your grades, I don't think you'll have a problem finding a good school to take you into their Pre Med program."

"I've tried to do my best," she announced proudly.

The counselor got up from her chair. "One of my student aides will show you around. She can help you locate your classes and your locker as well."

"Thank you, Mrs. Walters." Melody's stomach quivered as her unease returned. New classes . . .new kids. Will they like me?

The counselor put a reassuring arm around her as they walked out of her office and into the waiting area.

"Don't fret." Mrs. Walters patted Melody lightly on the back. "Your records show you did well in school and were liked by both students and teachers. I'm sure you'll fit in just fine here at River View and do just as well."

"I hope so."

"Annette," Mrs. Walters called to a petite, long-haired brunette who was busy filing student schedule cards.

Hearing her name, the student aide looked up from her duties.

"I need you to show Melody around school. She's new to River View. In fact, she's new to a lot of things. She's been schooling in London. But now back home. Let's see if we can make her feel welcome."

"Sure thing, Mrs. Walters." Annette closed the file cabinet, grabbed a new student packet from a shelf nearby and turned to Melody. "C'mon, follow me."

Melody followed Annette out of the guidance office and into the hallways of River View High. She was glad class was in session and it was quiet. Intently, she listened to everything Annette had to say. It was so much information to take in and remember. In addition to learning the basic layout of the school, she was also told about activities she could get involved in, clubs she could join, and the eating schedule. Annette's warm smile and bubbly personality put her at ease.

Annette paused in the center stairwell. "Did you really go to school in London?"

"Yes, I did. Why?"

"Because if my knowledge of geography is correct, London is not the warmest place in the world, and you've got a great tan for someone who's been living there."

Melody laughed and leaned back against the stair railing.

"Actually, I'm originally from Florida, but the reason for the great tan is that I spent the summer with my parents in Brazil."

"Brazil?" Annette's emerald eyes grew wide. "Are your parents loaded or something?"

"Yeah, I guess they are," Melody told Annette. "It's great. I get to experience so much. I've traveled to so many places."

"You're so lucky."

Melody grimaced, then frowned. "I'm sorry. I probably sound foolish bragging about my family's money."

Annette shook her head and smiled. "It's okay. Your life sounds interesting. I don't mind hearing about it."

Melody smiled back, feeling uneasy once more. "My dad inherited a lot of his wealth. But he still works hard to maintain it. Most of our trips are related to his business deals."

"It must be great to see so many different places." Annette sighed.

"It's not always fun and games. I was away at school most of the time, so I didn't see my family often. Now that I'm back with them, we don't really talk much. Sometimes I feel like I hardly know them. I'm close to my sister, though. Her name's Leigh, and she's twenty-four. Do you have any brothers or sisters?"

Annette nodded. "An older brother, Nick. But he's away right now in college."

"Leigh just graduated from college," Melody said. "It was her idea for me to come here. She said it was high time for me to go to school with boys."

"You went to an all-girls school?" Annette gasped, then giggled. "How could you stand it?"

Melody suddenly looked sad. "It's all I've ever known, so I don't feel as though I've missed anything."

"Hey, what's wrong?"

"Well, it's just that I don't know how to act here. I don't want people to think I'm stuck up just because my family has money."

"You seem like a very sweet and sincere person. I'm sure others will see that, too."

"Thank you, Annette. You've been a big help."

Annette looked at her watch. "I'd better get you to class. You've already missed two while you were getting registered."

Melody nodded. "I want to make a good impression, so I'd better not miss anymore."

"Let's see." Annette looked over Melody's schedule. "Room 115, English class with Mrs. Robertson. You'll like her. She's a great teacher. She can even make Shakespeare understandable and interesting."

Melody followed Annette to the correct room, where the two stopped in front of the closed door.

"Since you're new and I'm the only person you've met, you can sit with me at lunch if you'd like. I usually eat inside the cafeteria. The food's not too bad, and maybe I can introduce you to some other students."

"Sounds great," Melody replied as she and Annette entered the class. "I'd like to get to know you better. I have the feeling we're going to be great friends."

Adrian was so focused on his thoughts he nearly ran into Annette in the hall.

"Adrian, what are you doing skipping class right here in the hallway where you can get caught?"

"Don't call me that. You know I hate that name." He sneered at his cousin. She might be family, but still.

"Excuse me, Bolt, what are you doing?"

"Actually, I was hoping to find you. I need you to locate someone."

"It figures." Annette groaned. "You only look for me when you need something. Is it important?"

"Come off it, Annette. If it wasn't, would I come to you? No, I'd take care of it myself."

"Hey, chill out, Adrian—oops, I mean Bolt." Annette teased.

He balled up his fists.

"Hmm, so you want me to find someone . . .what's her name?"

"I don't know," he growled. Why does she have me figured out so well? "But she shouldn't be hard to find. She's obviously new. I never seen her before today. She showed up this morning driving a Porsche. Completely hot, too."

Annette put a hand on his shoulder. "Let me guess—blonde hair, blue eyes, about five-foot-seven, and wearing a hot-pink mini dress?"

"Yeah, with a fine, round ass and nice tits, too." Adrian grinned widely.

"Bolt!" Annette's eyes narrowed as she smacked him on the arm.

"Mmmm yes, the mini dress . . .that's her." Adrian licked his lips. "You've seen her?"

"Yes, I have, and so would you, if you were in class right now. She's got English this period, too."

"Fuck! I can't go to class now—Robertson would just throw me out, and I'd look stupid in front of the new chick."

Annette burst out laughing. "And when did you start caring what people think about you?"

"Come on, you saw how amazing she is."

"Yeah, so she caught your attention. Do you think you can catch hers? Your reputation with girls sucks around here."

"You love me."

"I'm family. I think it's required by law."

Adrian huffed. "That didn't stop your dad from throwing me out."

"Only because you acted like an obnoxious egomaniac," Annette reminded him. "And why should I even play matchmaker for you? Having a girlfriend has never been on your agenda."

"Who said anything about a girlfriend? I just want to . . ."

She slapped her hand over his mouth. "Don't even say it."

He pulled her hand down. "I was just gonna say I want to see her. Can't I look at a beautiful girl without you thinking I'm going to try to have sex with her?"

She sighed heavily. "Oh, so you're not going to try and have sex with her?"

"Well, not today. Tomorrow, who knows?"

Annette shook her head. "Look. I spoke with her for about half an hour and I can tell you, I doubt she'll give you the time of day. But since I have a soft spot for you, I'll help you out if I can."

"Ha! I knew you would."

He and Annette were polar opposites, but they had always been close. As little kids, they'd been inseparable. After his mom left, Annette had often been the one who comforted him when he was sad. When he'd moved in with her family, she'd always stood up for him when his uncle complained about his music, his clothes or his attitude.

"Her name is Melody Stewart, and if you really want to see her, she'll be having lunch with me in the cafeteria today."

"Thanks." Adrian grabbed her in his arms and hoisted her up. "You're the best."

"You sound serious about this one, Adrian."

"Bolt!" he corrected her again and set her back down. "I'm not serious at all. I just want to check her out some more. You see, it pleases me to look at her."

"I bet it does." Annette giggled softly. "I wonder if she'll say the same thing when she gets a look at you." Annette ran her fingers through Adrian's blond spikes.

Adrian pushed her hand away. "That's why I'm not serious. I saw her car, she's probably a stuck up bitch. However, you could put in a good word for me. Tell her what a sweet, wonderful guy I am."

"She is not stuck up. And she and I are becoming friends. What would she think if I started lying to her?"

Adrian scowled, but Annette just laughed. "I'm kidding.

But don't expect me to set you up on a date with her. That's your job. And if she says yes, then I expect you to live up to that sweet and wonderful crap."

"No problem." Adrian shrugged. "Just see if she notices me today and let me know what she thinks."

"Sure." Annette began to walk away. "Just remember, you owe me about a dozen favors."

Adrian waved goodbye. "See you around."

Adrian took off in the opposite direction, thinking of Melody. That short dress hugged every curve. Oh man—to hold that ass in my hands! His heart began pounding as he realized how soon he'd see her.

"Damn!" He groaned. "Here I go again."

He had to stay in control and not let this chick get to him. Yet, the thought of seeing her again filled him with a strange sense of euphoria he had never felt before.

Now the question is—what will she think of me?

About the Author

Cass Ford began creating smoldering male protagonists when she was five years old and convinced her aunt that she had a hot and heavy kindergarten boyfriend. In grade school, she penned tales on her parents' typewriter and by middle school sold her own love and gossip magazines to friends. As a preteen at sleepover camp, Cass often told playful, steamy bedtime stories to her bunkmates.

After earning her Bachelor of Journalism degree and several TV/film certificates, Cass continued to hone her passion for storytelling as a television producer. Born and raised in Canada, she now resides in California.

www.ingramcontent.com/pod-product-compliance
Lightning Source LLC
Chambersburg PA
CBHW070845120626
46556CB00002B/880